REVENGE ERA

BRITTANÉE NICOLE

CONTENTS

1. Lake   1
2. Ford   9
3. Lake   19
4. Ford   29
5. Lake   39
6. Ford   45
7. Lake   48
8. Ford   54
9. Lake   65
10. Lake   72
11. Ford   89
12. Lake   94
13. Ford   99
14. Lake   103
15. Ford   113
16. Lake   123
17. Ford   130
18. Lake   137
    Epilogue   144
19. Chapter 1 - Lake   150
20. Chapter 2 - Ford   153
21. Chapter 3 - Lake   156
22. Chapter 4 - Ford   161
23. Chapter 5 - Ford   165
24. Chapter 6 - Lake   173

    Sneak Peek of Trouble   177
    Acknowledgments   183
    Also by Brittanée Nicole   185

PLAYLIST

This is Why We Can't Have Nice Things

Getaway Car

Anti-Hero

Snow on the Beach (feat. Lana Del Ray)

I Knew You Were Trouble.

Blank Space

Dress

Dancing With Our Hands Tied

Look What You Made Me Do

Call it What You Want

I Did Something Bad

So It Goes...

Delicate

Paper Rings

Lavendar Haze

Wildest Dreams (Taylor's Version)

Daylight

Lover

Sweet Nothing

Eyes Open

The Archer

Don't Blame Me

Say Don't Go

So It Goes

Labyrinth

All Songs by Taylor Swift

LAKE
1

THIS IS WHY WE CAN'T HAVE NICE THINGS

"Are you ready for it?" Paul hands me a red package tied with fancy gold bows. He definitely had help with wrapping this.

Beaming at him, I grasp the box with both hands. It's too big for jewelry. Excitement bubbles inside me at the thought. Maybe he got creative with this year's Christmas present.

Admittedly, I'm not easy to shop for. Not because I'm picky in the least—I'd honestly be happy with a homemade gift. Or a small, meaningful memento. Christmas isn't about accumulating possessions. And regardless, if I want it, I can buy it myself. I don't need a man to do that for me.

But knowing that inside this box is something that Paul chose for me, a gift he spent his time thinking about, *that's* what matters most.

Paul's father Ford sits across from us on the couch, a whiskey in hand. He's stupidly good-looking, with dark hair that has just a hint of gray peppered throughout. He leans back like he owns the world, thighs wide and relaxed. As if he's a king surveying his kingdom. And what a beautiful kingdom it is. It's a cold one, though. Aside from the expertly decorated tree in the corner, all golds and blacks without a hint of personalization, there is not a single decoration in sight.

Blue eyes, which his son unfortunately did not inherit, observe me as I unwrap the present, careful not to rip the gorgeous paper.

Paul's phone beeps on the table, stealing his attention. He picks it up and types out a response. I wait for him to finish and set the device down again before sliding the white cardboard lid off and delicately pulling the gold paper aside. Anticipation has me sucking in a breath, but when I find a red scarf with the tag on it laid haphazardly inside, my lungs deflate.

Averting my focus from the price tag—I meant what I said, I don't expect extravagance—I lift it up and smile. "A scarf. Thank you so much."

Across from me, the couch squeaks as Ford sits up and rests his hands on his knees. His attention is almost suffocating. Although you'd think I'd be used to it by now. Eyes always on me. A camera always ready to capture my reaction. I hope my smile appears genuine. That my disappointment isn't obvious.

It's not that a scarf isn't a perfectly good gift. A hand-knit scarf? I'd be over the moon. A scarf purchased during Paul's travels because he was thinking of me? Totally swoon worthy. But as my eyes snag on the two-for-one tag that states this item came with a hat, my heart sinks a bit. Because there is no hat.

"Since red is your favorite color," Paul says.

Yes, I'm known for the color. I wear it during every show, it colors my lips, and a few of my songs even include lyrical nods to that. But shouldn't my boyfriend of two years know more about me than my fans?

Every day I receive red items from people who want to send me gifts. I've probably even received a scarf or two in the last week.

Maybe that gift-giver also sent the matching hat.

Don't be selfish. This is what money and fame do. They tear people apart. Paul put thought into this gift, and that's all that matters. We're traveling in the cold over the next week, so a scarf is a logical gift.

I lean over and press my red lips against his cheek. "Thank you, baby."

He grins and nods at his dad. "You going to open your gift?"

Ford doesn't take his eyes off me as he brings his whiskey to his lips. He probably thinks I'm an asshole for not being more excited about my gift. With his jaw locked tight, he sets his glass down and picks up the present Paul set in front of him moments ago. Unlike me, he doesn't take his time to preserve the paper as he pulls out a red hat with a pom-pom.

"Oh look, it matches your scarf," Ford drolls. I can't tell if he's aware that they were an actual matching set.

I offer my famous Lake Paige smile, the one that shows all my teeth, and make sure my eyes are bright. "Perfect."

Paul fiddles with the watch I picked out for him for Christmas and taps my foot. "You ready to head out?"

Ford clears his throat. "Thank you for joining me for lunch. I know with the tour picking up again tonight that your schedule is packed."

I take a deep breath and nod. The tour. Right.

Since I was a teenager, I've spent at least one holiday a year traveling. My birthday, my parents' birthdays, Thanksgiving, Christmas. You name it, and I've spent it singing to stadiums packed with people chanting my name.

This is the first year that I have someone by my side for all of it, though. Someone to enjoy the madness, the crazy, and the quiet. We're halfway through the world tour for my seventh album, and Paul has been by my side for every show so far. Ford's label produced my last two albums. It's how Paul and I met.

When the tour schedule was finalized and we realized I only had three days off between locations, Paul offered to come with me so we wouldn't have to do long distance. My heart aches at the thought. He's given up so much for me. He quit his job to be close to me. Of course he can't afford more than a scarf if he doesn't want to use his father's credit card.

Not that he doesn't use the black card regularly.

Dropping my chin, I shake my head. I like that he scrounged up his own money to pay for my gift. That, for once, he didn't rely on his father.

"You coming tonight?" I ask Ford as he helps me into my black coat.

He lifts my long brown hair from beneath the collar and settles it against my shoulder, his touch featherlight and quick. Always respectful.

My boyfriend laughs. "Oh, Daddy Ford is busy. You're not his only artist, you know."

I turn around just in time to watch as Ford's jaw flexes. "How many times do I have to tell you not to call me that?"

The women in his office at the label fawn over the man. I get it. He could definitely be categorized as a Daddy.

That's just not my thing.

I'm the good girl with long brown hair and a bright, red-lipped smile at all times. And Paul, with his windswept blond hair, looks great next to me.

Our photos are splashed across the covers of almost every magazine, even when I wish they weren't. But Paul does well with the attention. Maybe even calls for it more often than I would like.

Ford leans in and brushes a kiss against my cheek. "Thank you for coming over and spending time with me," he says, looking from me to Paul and back again. "I have a hockey game tonight, but we both know Clay has everything covered." With his hands stuffed in his pockets, he steps back and winks.

I tuck my chin to hide the blush creeping up my cheeks. "As he always does."

In fact, my tour manager is likely losing his mind right now. I can picture him running around like mad, making sure every one of the million things that have to be completed at the last minute are done perfectly. I do a surprise song at every show, and tonight's is fitting for the holidays. I'll be dancing on top of an oversized glass of champagne, and the crew will be spraying the audience with bottles of bubbly.

Those lucky enough to have scored seats in the first few rows, at least.

Clay grumbled about wasting the good bubbly, but I'm certainly not shooting cheap champagne at my fans.

Buttons, Ford's black cat, brushes against my leg, and I lean down to rub her head. The sound and steady vibration of her purring calms me just a little. I've been doing this for years, yet nerves still hit me before every show.

Paul sighs. "I told you I'm allergic. Don't touch that thing."

"You're not allergic," Ford snorts. "You just listen to everything your mother says, and because she hates cats, you do too."

My heart sinks. I miss my cat fiercely, but when Paul said he was allergic, I asked my mother to take her.

Speechless, I follow an aggravated Paul out the door. With a wave to Ford, I make my way into the cold. His house is an hour outside Boston in a small town on the water. During scheduling, I insisted our holiday shows take place in Boston and New York so we could celebrate with our families.

Early on in my career, I ate up the California sunshine and the LA lifestyle, but now I can't step outside my apartment without being recognized and followed. Flying under the radar on the East Coast, especially the smaller towns like this one, has been such a relief.

Paul doesn't even look at our driver when he nods at him, but I stop and chat because that's what I do. I don't take this life for granted, and I don't want people to think I do. If I'm not overly friendly with staff, even when I'm too tired to think, then weeks later, rumors will fly that I was rude or inconsiderate. It happened far too often during those first few years, so I now go out of my way to be friendly.

As a woman, I don't get to have a bad day.

When I finally slide in next to Paul, his eyes are closed and he's already got his headphones on. He says he needs to rest before shows. He needs the quiet time to zone out because they can be so chaotic. I don't blame him. My life is kind of a circus. And truth be told, I'm exhausted too. We've spent the last few days bouncing between our families.

Ford's was by far the most relaxed visit we've had. We spent

Christmas Eve with my family, where it felt like the entire town was present. On Christmas morning, we drove north to Paul's mother's house. His brother and sister, Daniel and Millie, were there as well. It had been a while since I'd seen the twins last, and their company is always welcome. Even if their mother requested I perform a little show for her family. And by family, she apparently meant every person she knows.

But it's fine. I didn't mind. I kept my signature smile in place and made the best of it. Ford suggested a quiet lunch, and I couldn't have been more thrilled about it.

Until the show starts, I won't use my vocal cords again, so I tip my head back, close my eyes, and try to relax. There isn't a lot I can control in my life, but when I'm on stage, nothing else really matters.

WITH A BOTTLE of water in my hand, I stride down one hall, then another. I'm covered in a mixture of sweat and champagne as I slap hands with every stagehand, assistant, dancer, and member of the support team I pass. The energy is always high after a show, but tonight is even crazier. The last number was a hit, just like I imagined it would be.

Still riding the wave of excitement, I'm on a mission to find Paul. We've been going nonstop for the last few weeks, and it'd be nice to have a little late Christmas celebration. Just us two.

I'll grab one of the bottles of champagne, get a shower in, and then surprise him with some solo attention.

The door to Clay's office is ajar, and I spy a few of the bottles just inside. I press the door open farther and step inside the darkened room so I can snag one, but before I can spin on my heel and continue on, a grunted "fuck" stops me.

On the other side of the open door, Clay is standing, chin tipped up, with a long-stemmed black bottle held out in front of him.

Ready to tease him for drinking one after making such a big show of how we were wasting money on the champagne, I take another step into the room. Only when I do, I get a glimpse of what's really going on in here.

He's not alone. I squeeze my eyes shut when I notice that Clay's pants are at his ankles and there's a guy on his knees in front of him.

I cover my eyes with my hand but spread my fingers a little so I can see the floor to make my way out. When he grunts, though, my gaze flies up to make sure he hasn't spotted me, and I watch as he tips his head back and pours my fancy champagne down his throat, then thrusts into his boyfriend's mouth. Fuck, I shouldn't be here. I must get out of here. Before I can make a silent escape, Clay's partner fists his cock, and the watch on his wrist snags my attention.

Why does it look familiar?

"Oh shit!" Clay gasps, pulling back from his partner's mouth, making his dick bob violently.

"Sorry!" I mutter. My feet aren't working and my brain has lost all control over my body, so I'm frozen in place, gaping like an idiot. The person on his knees slaps his hands to the floor for balance, and that's when my brain starts to work again. And I realize *why* I recognize that watch.

It's the one I gave Paul this afternoon.

My stomach drops as my boyfriend shuffles back and whips his head in my direction.

For a moment, he sputters, his eyes wide and his face twisted into a horrified expression. "Lake, I can explain!" he says, clambering to his feet.

I open my mouth, but I can't find the words.

"It's not what you think," Paul mutters, smoothing his hair.

With my lungs squeezing so tight I can't breathe, I look from Clay, who is stumbling as he tries to pull up his pants, to Paul, who is wiping at his mouth.

"It's not what I think?" I finally ask, shaking off the shock and turning to the appropriate emotion. *Rage.* "You had his dick in your mouth, and it's *not what I think*? You cheated on me!" I hiss, finally finding my backbone.

Paul's blond hair flops as he shakes his head. "No. He's a man, babe." He reaches for me. "It's not like that."

"Oh my God," I say, lurching back before he touches me.

Clay's response is an echo of mine.

My vision tunnels and rage courses through me. My body is on fire. Hotter than it was at the end of my two-and-a-half-hour show. My hands shake as I reach for the bottle of champagne Clay dropped on the table in his haste to put on his pants.

"I'll be taking this," I grit out. It takes everything in me not to scream so I don't fuck up my vocal cords. He's so not worth it. "You can keep him, though." I point the neck of the bottle at Paul, then bring it to my lips and tip it back. On the way out the door, I throw a middle finger over my shoulder. "Oh, and Clay?" I say, spinning quickly.

An expression of hope crosses the audacious fucker's face, making this moment even sweeter for me.

Pulling my shoulders back, I revel in snuffing out the light in his eyes. "In case you haven't figured it out yet, you're fucking fired!"

FORD

2

GETAWAY CAR

"**M**y man." Gavin Langfield claps me on the back and pulls me in for a half hug when he steps into the owner's suite at Bolts' Arena. My best friend's family owns the hockey team, and a few of his brothers even play.

"Merry Christmas," I say as I pull back.

He grins. "Merry Christmas it is. My team is killing it, and my best friend is about to tell me his superstar son is finally going to come play for us."

A laugh bubbles out of me. "You know the rules."

Gavin drafted Daniel when he was eighteen. Pro hockey differs from most other sports in this way. A team like the Bolts can draft a player in college but then allow him to remain in school and play in the NCAA league. Once the player has reached their pinnacle level, according to the team, at least, a contract is offered. From there, he'd leave college for the minors or maybe even the NHL. Daniel hit that level when he was nineteen, and Gavin's been on my ass to bring him up to the NHL ever since.

But college is important to me. My kids will never worry about money, so Daniel doesn't need the contract. What he needs is a fucking degree. Something I know will go by the wayside the minute he starts playing for the NHL. Though it's wildly unorthodox, and to outsiders, probably a poor decision on his part, out of respect for me, Gavin has never spoken to Daniel about bringing him up.

This is the one thing I still have control over when it comes to my kids. Daniel and his twin sister are twenty-two, and in general, they do what they want. Just like Paul.

The twins spent Christmas with their mother this year. It's easier that way. She's good at getting what she wants, and they know I understand. I spent time with them last week, and we have plans to get together again before they go back to school. The only reason Paul made an appearance today is because of Lake. She's thoughtful in a way that's almost detrimental to her. She goes out of her way to make those around her feel happy, appreciated, welcome. She couldn't stand the idea of me being alone for the holiday and scheduled a trip to see me so I could spend the day after Christmas with my son. Or lunch, at least.

Hey, it's something.

Gavin motions to the seats in the front. Like me, he doesn't like to miss a minute of the game. The fancy bar and the food in the suite don't interest us. "How's Millie?"

"Perfect, as always."

Gavin laughs. "What's her plan after college?"

"If it were up to me, she'd intern with the label, but she's always wanted to go her own way. And she's Daniel's shadow. I don't know what she'll do when he signs that contract and she can't make it to every one of his games. She's his biggest fan."

"Smart girl. The boy is a beast on skates."

My chest warms. "Don't I know it."

"And Paul?"

A waitress approaches us before I can answer, but once we've each ordered a glass of Hanson whiskey and she leaves us, I let my shoulders slump and sigh. "Paul is Paul. Just as selfish and lazy as ever. I have no idea how Lake stays with him."

Gavin raises his brows. "He's lucky, isn't he? Landed the hottest act around."

A fire ignites in my veins at that, and I have to lock my jaw to keep from biting my friend's head off. I despise the way people talk about her like she's nothing but a pretty face. The talent that girl has in her pinky surpasses every other artist I've ever signed. She's also smart and kind. Too kind sometimes.

Like today. There's no way she didn't notice that her boyfriend bought a generic hat and scarf set and gave us each one piece for Christmas. Paul didn't even bother to buy his girlfriend her own gift. Fuck, I thought I raised him better.

More and more, I'm realizing we didn't do a great job of raising him at all. The twins, though, always have one another's backs. They're thoughtful and they care about all of us. But they were still so young when Kyla and I split. By the time they were old enough to understand what was going on, she and I had figured out how to be friends and good co-parents. And money was flowing a bit easier by then, too.

Truth is, both of my boys are a little spoiled. Can't say the same about Millie, though. I will accept no complaints regarding my perfect daughter.

Like Lake, she deserves all the protection.

More than a little eager to change the subject, I lean forward and rest my elbows on my knees. "Seeing anyone?"

Gavin smirks. "Sure, I see a lot of ones."

That gets a laugh out of me. That's pure Gavin. Not the least bit interested in settling down, but always up for a fun time.

"What are you two laughing about?" his brother Beckett grumps from a few seats down. Like the two of us, Beckett's true focus is on the game. While he's the owner of Boston's most successful baseball team, the Revs, he's always been good at supporting his brothers.

"Just Gav's inability to settle down."

"Says the guy who hasn't been in a relationship since his kids were in diapers," Gavin snorts.

All I can do is shrug. I lost interest in that kind of thing after my divorce. Sure, I spend the night with women here and there and even see a few of them occasionally because I enjoy company at dinners and award shows, but if I've learned one thing in the last twenty years or so, it's that there isn't a woman out there who gets me. A woman I'm willing to compromise for, who makes me want to give up nights with the boys to just hang with her.

"At least I'm done with the kid thing. You two still have that to look forward to."

Gavin throws his head back and snorts. "Can you imagine Beckett with a kid?"

Beckett rolls his eyes. "I don't want kids, so your insults won't affect me."

"Eh," I say. "You'll change your tune when you meet the woman of your dreams." Even though Kyla and I didn't work out, I'll never regret becoming a father. At forty-seven, my days of raising kids are long gone. But I've got a few years on my friends. They still have time to do all that.

Gavin grins. "My brother already met the love of his life. She just doesn't know he exists."

Beckett growls. "What the hell are you talking about?"

Gavin laughs like an idiot and takes the whiskey from the server when she appears. Then he taps his glass against mine. "To Olivia Maxwell, the only woman Beckett will ever want."

His brother rolls his eyes. "She works for us," he says to me. "And she's married."

Shaking my head at their theatrics, I sit back and settle in for the game. I spend the next ninety minutes watching the action on the ice and texting back and forth with Daniel. He goes on and on about wanting to come with me the next time I'm hanging with the Langfield brothers, and I promise to bring him up to Boston in the New Year. Just gotta come up with some threats ahead of time to keep Gavin from chirping in his ear. Otherwise the kid will leave his last semester of college so he can be here for the playoffs.

I'm just slipping my phone back into my pocket when it buzzes in my hand, so I pull it out again. Shit. My assistant's name flashes on the screen, which means I absolutely can't ignore it. I'm a hands-on boss and keep tabs on my artists and what they're up to at all times, so I'm usually the one checking in, not the other way around. If Lisa is calling me, it's because there's a problem.

"You need to get to Bar 31." No *hello*, no *we've got a problem*. Lisa gets right to it.

With a nod to the guys, I stand and head out. They get it. The Langfields run two of Boston's most prolific sports teams. They understand that one phone call could signal a million disasters. Disasters that could cost millions in only minutes if not dealt with quickly.

My gut tells me this phone call is exactly that.

"Who's at Bar 31?"

She taps at her phone, the sound beating against my ear. I pull it back and scowl as I wait for her to answer my question.

"Sorry." She types for another few seconds, then rapid-fires the facts. "Lake. She caught Paul sucking Clay off after the show. Took a bottle of champagne and made a big show of it. Then she comman-deered one of the backup dancers, who snuck her into an Uber. Now she's dancing on the bar top at Bar 31. It's all over the internet."

"Fuck." My stomach drops. "The vultures already found her?"

Lisa laughs. It's breathy and filled with sarcasm. "TikTok and Instagram, Daddy Ford. These days, everybody's a vulture. Teeny boppers with iPhones get the scoop long before the paps ever do."

My heart rate picks up. She's right. Maybe my first thought should be about my son. I had no idea he was into men. Or a cheater. Maybe a good parent would focus on their child. But honestly, I barely consider the implications. Because Lake *is* my label. We took a risk on her a few years ago, and it's paid off one hundred–fold. She's the reason each of my kids has a black card and every luxury they could think of. It's why Paul, the lazy ass, is even here. Because of *her* success, he's living the high life.

My phone pings in my ear, so I pull it away and click on the video Lisa shared. "What the fuck?" I growl.

Lake hasn't even changed out of the glittery outfit she wore for the closing number. Once I'm in the hallway outside the owner's suite, I slump against the concrete wall and watch the train wreck on the six-inch screen. My grip on the phone tightens as the camera pans up her long, creamy legs. Legs everyone is commenting on.

She is strikingly beautiful.

When the camera hits her wide hips, I grind my teeth.

Move the camera up, fucker.

The image wobbles like the person recording stumbled or got jostled by others trying to get closer to Lake. When the video gets clear again, it's focused on her breasts. The gold sequin leotard shimmers as she heaves in breaths. The shiny material only accentuates a pair of tits I've never focused on, even as I approved or rejected outfit ideas for shows or an album cover. Even if I had looked a few seconds too long, I never would have been graced with a view like this. Lake is the good girl of music. Fans expect a certain look. This number was chosen for this holiday set. It's far more revealing than anything the pop princess would normally wear.

Jesus, her father is going to kill me for okaying this.

Did I okay this?

When the camera hits her face, I don't zero in on her lips, where I'm sure the rest of America is focused. Those red lips are famous.

No, my gaze zeroes in on her eyes. Vacant. Completely devoid of emotion.

The girl is so used to hiding her feelings she doesn't even have to practice the look.

She's clearly close to breaking down. To the rest of the world, her smile looks bright and she looks like she's having the time of her life, but this is a façade. When Lake smiles for the cameras, her eyes always convey how appreciative she is for all she has.

To be clear, she's earned it. Every single dollar, every single award, and every single fan. No one works harder than her.

But she always makes sure to express her gratitude.

Right now, though, she isn't faking anything. While her lips tell one story, bright and cheery and ready to sing a big fuck-you to my son, her eyes are hauntingly empty.

And fuck me if I don't decide in that moment that I'll do anything to fix that.

HOLDING my jacket tight against my body, I weave my way through the crowd. The bouncer, who was warned of my arrival, holds open the door for me. As I hustle inside, the guys in the front of the line groan. "Really? Who the hell is this guy?"

I ignore them. My focus fixed solely on finding Lake and getting her out of here without too much fanfare. It only takes an instant to spot her in the crowded club. She's still on the bar top, sparkling like a fucking disco ball.

Fuck me. I bite my fist and rack my brain for a plan of action while forcing myself to ignore the urge to study every inch of her body. Starting with those damn legs and thick thighs. I've never been so entranced by her curves. It must be the fucking outfit.

When I remember the vacancy in her eyes in the video, my feet move.

Shouldering my way through the crowd, I head straight for the bar. I can't quite push my way past the two men standing below her with their cameras pointed between her legs, but thankfully her friend spots me. "Looks like you're in trouble, Lake. Daddy's here!"

I cringe at the damn nickname, but at least it makes the guys push back in response to the comment. They probably think I'm her actual father. Can't think about that too long.

"She's right. Fun's over." I push forward and hold my hand out to her.

She sways away before I can grasp her arm. "Oh, Daddy Ford," she slurs from above me, "you here to clean up Pauly's mess? He's been a bad boy." Fuck. She's way past drunk. With a seductive smirk, she brings one finger to her red lips. "Although, I guess I've been bad too. You going to put me over your knee and spank me?"

Her friend laughs, a bright and bubbly sound, and Lake brightens like she's proud of herself.

"I'm sorry my son is an ass. We'll deal with him, I promise. But right now, we need to get you out of here before the rest of Boston shows up."

Throwing her arms up and tossing her head back, Lake yells, "You hear that, Boston? The man says y'all want more of me! Everyone wants me!"

The crowd cheers in response, and, encouraged by their glee, she takes a little bow. She wraps one arm around her midsection and holds the other out, then tips forward, but she overextends and stumbles, losing her footing. I grab her and toss her over my shoulder, and without hesitation, I rush toward the exit ahead of the swarming crowd.

"Fucking A!" she screeches as she pounds against my back. "*Put me down.*"

A laugh breaks free from my chest. I've never heard Lake curse, and it's sexy as fuck coming out of her perfect little mouth. "Not a chance."

She blows out a frustrated breath against my back. "At least the view isn't terrible."

"Huh?" I question over the music as I haul ass out of the club.

At the door, my driver is waiting to direct us to the car and help keep bystanders from approaching.

As soon as we hit the cold Boston air, she hisses. "Shit, it's cold."

With a sigh, I set her on her feet and hold her elbows until she's steady. Then I shuck my coat and wrap her in it. "What view?"

She smiles and stands tall, only wobbling a little. "Your ass. I've never really paid attention before, but for an old man, you've got a nice one."

"Old man?" I grind out.

She smiles. "Don't worry, I like everyone. Equal opportunist and all that. Even asses. Just ask your son."

Pinching the bridge of my nose, I close my eyes and try to make sense of what she's saying. She's heartbroken and drunk, though, so it's not likely I will. And it doesn't matter whether she thinks I'm an old man or not. Truth is, I am, at least compared to her.

Fuck, none of this matters. My only concern should be getting her to her hotel before the crowds descend on this bar.

"My son's an idiot." I point to the passenger door Anders is holding open.

Her shoulders slump, and she drops her chin, but she looks at me from under the fake lashes that are still in place from this evening's show. "Thanks for saving me. And I'm sorry. I probably ruined your plans and made your life exceedingly more complicated, since now you'll have to clean up my mess as well as Paul's."

This girl. Even after my son cheated on her and my employee caused her pain, she's apologizing to me. Fuck, always trying to say the right thing must be exhausting. I'm worn out just listening to her.

"Get in the car, Lake. And stop apologizing." I hold my arm out to the open passenger door again.

With a long breath out, she finally turns. When she notices the Ferrari, she squeaks and whips around again. This time, her smile is a real one. "Oh, can I drive?"

I glare at her. "You're drunk. And when was the last time you drove?"

She bites hard on her plump lower lip and whispers, "A long fucking time."

I herd her toward the car and do my best to block the view of people hovering nearby with their phones out. "Sit. If you're good, maybe I'll let you drive her tomorrow."

A look of giddy surprise glitters across her face, and her eyes brighten. "Really?"

The tightness in my chest eases a fraction, and I let out a light laugh. "Really. Now will you please get in the fucking car? The paps will be rolling up here any second."

She does a little shimmy and claps, and then she's scooting inside.

I give Anders a look, and that's all it takes for him to pull out his phone. He'll order an Uber. As I round the car, she leans over to make sure my door is unlocked. The simple move has my swallow heavy. She's always watching out for everyone else, always doing little things to make sure the people around her are taken care of. A weight settles on me, bringing with it a need to do the same for her. To show her precisely how she deserves to be treated. To encourage her to just fucking relax for ten seconds without worrying about anyone but herself.

But that heavy feeling doesn't last, because when I get in the car, Lake is already fiddling with the radio. By the time I have my seat belt on, the music is blasting and she's bouncing in her seat. I don't argue, because at the same time, a van with no windows in the back pulls up. That's our cue to get the fuck out of Dodge.

With a wicked smirk, she cocks a brow at me and says, "Guess you're driving the getaway car."

LAKE
3

ANTI-HERO

As Ford takes off down the highway, the rumble of the engine sends a burst of electricity sliding down my legs and straight to my toes. My stomach flips when he turns and smiles at me. It's a devilish smile. A wicked one. Like we're in on some crazy secret.

For a moment, I relish it. The wind from the open window leaves my hair swirling around me—the night is cold, but the frigid air is cleansing. Cathartic. The loud music pulsing through the car. The scent surrounding me. The car smells like man, like masculine woodsy cologne.

He's nothing like Paul.

That little thought causes warning bells to go off in my brain. I shouldn't be enjoying this. Ford isn't sitting beside me because I'm out on some secret escapade. He's here because his son fucked around on me. And because I lost my damn mind and made a scene.

He's merely doing his job as head of the record label. He's cleaning up the mess.

I sink into the seat, turn my head toward the window, and close my eyes.

Far too quickly, we're pulling up in front of my hotel. The sight makes my stomach drop. There isn't another car or person around, but the last time I was here, I was stepping out these doors with Paul.

"Paul isn't here. And if you want, we can move your things to another room."

Embarrassment burns at the backs of my eyes, so I keep my face turned toward the passenger window. "Thanks," I try to whisper, but the word barely makes it past the giant lump in my throat. I tilt my face down so my hair falls around it like a curtain and reach for the door handle, but I freeze when his warm palm lands on my thigh.

The touch seers me into a trance. Still hiding behind my hair, I suck in a breath as my eyes fly to where he grips my bare skin. It's indecent-looking, his massive hand, tan and just a little weathered with age, against the pale skin of my upper thigh.

"Don't move," he instructs, as if he has no idea that his touch alone has left me paralyzed.

Obviously the contact had no effect on him. Naïve little Lake, always feeling too much, thinking too much, while the men around me just take and take and take.

He removes his hand, but I keep my focus trained on the space he just touched, wondering if it will look as branded as I suddenly feel. When he opens my door and holds out his hand, I have to shake myself from the haze that's settled over me.

He's your boyfriend's father.

Ex-boyfriend, the devil on my shoulder taunts. It goes without saying the relationship was over the moment I found him sucking Clay's cock.

The thought leaves me shivering.

Ford must think I'm cold, because he wraps an arm around me and pulls me to his side. "Let's get you warmed up in your room."

The fight has left me. The night's events hit me all at once, like one punch to the gut after another, so I lean against his chest and allow him to lead me through the foyer.

Like magic, a woman wearing a name tag I don't bother to read appears, holding out two key cards. She avoids glancing in my direction as she addresses Ford. "Both rooms are available. Let us know if we can do anything else to make your stay more comfortable, Mr. Hall."

With a quick thanks, he guides me toward the elevator, scanning our surroundings as if he's looking for reporters or paps. Not that either is necessary for a photo leak. Every person we encountered on our way out of the bar likely has a phone. Tomorrow's story will probably imply that I cheated on Paul with his dad.

The irony.

I let out a heavy breath once the stainless-steel doors of the elevator slide closed. We made it, sight unseen, *hopefully*. Pressing my back against the cool metal wall, I shuffle to one side, distancing myself from the man that is currently dominating my thoughts.

"Which room do you want?" he asks, holding up the two cards. Unlike the woman, at least he realizes this is my choice. "The second suite is almost the size of the one you've been staying in."

"I'll stay where I was. All my stuff is there."

He holds out one card, then pockets the other. When I step off the elevator, I turn to thank him, but he's already following me off.

"Is your room on this floor too?" As far as I know, my suite takes up most of this level.

Ford frowns and takes a step closer. "I don't have a room."

Right. Why would he be staying here? His house is only an hour from Boston. He'll probably just return the key when he leaves.

I sidestep him to catch the elevator door before it closes. "You don't have to walk me to my room. I promise I won't go back out."

An exasperated breath leaves him, and he puts a hand to my hip and guides me down the hall. "Just let me take care of you tonight, okay?"

Jumbled thoughts rush together again as his proximity and words leave me dizzy. He can't possibly plan to—

Okay, yes, he is walking me to my door. As I stare stupidly at him, he takes the key I'm still holding and slaps it against the sensor above the handle. When the light flashes green, he pushes the door open and ushers me inside.

Ford doesn't stop moving. He walks straight through the living area, passing the kitchenette and the seating area and the gorgeous view of the Boston skyline out the floor-to-ceiling windows until we're standing outside the double doors that lead to the bedroom. He pulls them open, then spins around and steps around me. "It's all set."

Confused and exhausted and still slightly buzzed—okay, majorly buzzed—I take a tentative step into the room, but wobble on my heels. Ford is by my side and catching me before I can tell him I'm fine.

He grumbles and points to the couch. "Let me help you get these off."

My clothes?

"The buckles on the heels. You'll fall over trying to get out of them."

Right. Of course he's not asking me to take my clothes off in front of him. That'd be insane.

I swat at his hand, determined to deal with it myself, but stumble again as I do.

Without another word, he grasps my hips and manhandles me, practically lifting me off the ground as he steers me toward the couch. He feels so much bigger right now. Or maybe the night has made me smaller. Like my stature shrank right along with my spirit.

"You promised you'd listen," he says with a tick of his jaw and his brow cocked up at me.

I let out a long breath. "To not going out. Not to all your orders. You're not my father."

"Thank god for that."

"Excuse me?" My pulse beats wildly at his remark. Maybe this isn't my finest moment, but he spawned the asshat who caused all of this.

Ford sighs and takes a step back. "That's not what I meant. Just—could you please sit down so I can help you?"

I narrow my eyes at him, but I'm too tired to argue, so I obey. But as soon as I settle on the couch, I go for the clasp of one shoe.

The growl that emanates from the man in front of me makes me freeze on the spot.

"Did you just growl at me?"

Kneeling, he grasps my foot and makes quick work of the buckle. Then he switches to the other one. When he finishes, he doesn't release my ankle. With a heavy breath and with his attention still locked on my foot, he says, "I'm trying to do the right thing. My son was a bastard, and you deserve better." He brushes his thumb over my ankle in the gentlest caress. "Please go into your room, take off this outfit, and go to bed."

I bite my lip and pull in an unsteady breath. What the hell is going on? He looks... tortured. Still clutching my ankle and refusing to look at me. The gravel in his tone. The way his chest rises and falls as if he's having trouble getting enough air.

"I need my foot to do that," I say, trying to break the tension.

He drops it immediately and shifts out of my way, but he still doesn't look at me. As I reach the double doors, I peer over my shoulder and find he's still kneeling on the floor beside the couch, his palm on the table as if he needs the support.

"Thank you for rescuing me. I'll do better tomorrow."

His shoulders rise and fall once before he pushes himself up and finally turns my way, stuffing his hands into his pockets. "You were perfect, Lake. You're always perfect." The words are flattering, but the look in his eye is one of pure disappointment. An instant later, he turns toward the skyline, and I take that as my cue that I'm dismissed.

As I scrub off my makeup, I'm struck by just how quiet it is. The buzz in my ears from the concert is still so loud it almost drowns out my thoughts. After hours in front of a crowd, with constant shadows attending to my every need, I should relish the peace. Instead, the silence highlights how truly alone I am. Not a single person except the head of my label was around to pick up the pieces when my life fell apart. And Ford is only here because I make him a lot of money.

It's his job to care.

His job to make sure I go back to being the perfect girl who always says the right things and acts the right way.

And it'll be his job to find a way to spin his son's actions.

On instinct, I suck in a harsh breath to stop the sob climbing up my throat from consuming me. Then, on second thought, I let my body take over. I lurch forward and slap my palms against the marble counter, giving my reflection a long, hard look. My red-rimmed eyes, the mascara streaking down my cheeks, my limp hair sticky with champagne. Why the hell am I trying to hold it all together? No one is here to witness my breakdown. I'm alone. Like always.

In a room of people, even when they're screaming my name, I'm always alone. No one is ever truly there for me. They come for the singer, the entertainer. Everyone wants her and what she can provide. I'm the show, nothing more.

For once, I want someone who wants *me*, the woman under the makeup and far from the spotlight, with all my faults and insecurities. Shutting off the light, I take a deep breath and shuffle into the bedroom, then I climb into my bed, pull the covers over my head, and cry.

A LOW RUMBLE WAKES ME. From the sound of the loud hissing coming from one of the rooms near mine, whoever it is must be pissed. I swipe the sleep from my eyes and crack an eye open. The light in the room is blinding, making my head pound. I pull the sheet over my head and blink a few times to wake myself up. Between the effects of the alcohol and the crying, today is going to suck.

At the sound of another angry rumble followed by a few low curses, I turn over in bed and face the opposite direction.

As I'm sliding the pillow over my head to block out the noise, I spot the aspirin and bottle of water on the bedside table.

Hmm. I don't remember putting that there.

I snag the water, noting how cool it is. Like it hasn't been sitting for long. Pushing that thought aside, I haul myself up against the head-board and take a sip, then pop the aspirin into my mouth too.

"This isn't a fucking vacation," the voice growls.

Damn, the angry man's voice is so close it sounds like it's coming from my suite. This is ridiculous.

I throw the comforter back and jump out of bed, stomping as I go. Maybe if I make a lot of noise, the person who broke into my room will get scared and run out. I grasp both handles and yank, pulling the double doors open so hard they slam into the walls on either side, and immediately let out a loud scream.

There's a man sitting on my couch.

Why am I screaming? I knew I wasn't alone. Logically I should not be freaking out right now. Okay, maybe I should be, but I should be freaking out from inside the locked bathroom while I call security. I should not have opened this damn door.

The man raises his head, and when he does, his eyes bug out and his jaw drops.

My screams finally come to a stop as I realize it's Paul's father, not a stranger.

Ford Hall.

Otherwise known as my boss.

Kind of.

Whoever he is to me, he's not someone I want to be screaming at in my hotel room at eight a.m.

"Shit, I gotta go." He hangs up the phone and stands, running a hand over the front of his rumpled pants. Pants I'm pretty sure he wore last night. The blue shirt is familiar too. The scruffy face and tired eyes are new, and his dark hair threaded with just a hint of gray has never looked this mussed.

"Did you…" I blink at him and point at the couch. "Did you sleep here?"

Ford Hall doesn't do sheepish, so he doesn't shrink back under my interrogation. He simply nods at the table. "Didn't want you to be alone. Ordered breakfast. I'm sure you're hungry after last night."

Starving, in fact, but I'm far too embarrassed by what he witnessed last night, and now I'm stuck on what he just said.

Didn't want me to be alone?

My manners kick in, finally, and command my next words. "I'm sorry. I didn't mean to ruin your night and make you sleep on the couch."

With a shake of his head, he settles back against the cushion. "Just eat. I'm fine."

What I should do is shower before the entire PR team walks in here. "When will Samantha be here?" I ask as I play with the necklace I must have forgotten to remove last night.

Ford's only response is a frown.

"Oh shit. Is this worse than Samantha? Is Lisa on her way?" Lisa is Ford's number two. She's probably working this already.

"Why would they come here?"

My stomach twists as blurry images of last night float through my mind. "I'm sure my phone is blowing up. I made a huge scene. So what are we doing to fix this?"

"Nothing," Ford says, draping one arm along the back of the couch, as if it's that simple.

My heart lurches at that. Why isn't he yelling at me? "Huh?"

"My son fucked up. He's going to own it." His glare is back, but it's aimed at his phone now.

"Your son doesn't own anything unless someone buys it for him."

He dips his chin and grumbles words I don't understand, but my stomach chooses that moment to growl, so I give up in favor of food.

"I don't drink coffee," I remind him when I see the carafe in the middle of the breakfast spread. I'm being bitchy, but my patience is all used up. I'm annoyed at Paul, absolutely, but I'm also annoyed at Ford. How can he act like this isn't a big deal? I can only imagine the field day the press is having. We should have been up and working with the PR team before dawn.

Without looking up from his phone, he says, "I had them bring chai tea and chocolate milk. Help yourself to whatever you want."

How did he know that's what I drink? My heart beats out an irregular rhythm at the thought that he noticed something so simple.

I pick up the cup of tea and take a sip. The hum of approval slips from me before I can stop it. It only takes a few seconds for my heart to steady, and I remember my manners. I spin and pull my shoulders back, set on fixing my otherwise bad behavior. "Thank you for the tea. And breakfast. I'm sorry for biting your head off."

Ford blinks at his phone and taps what appears to be another angry message into it. Then he pockets it and looks up at me. This time his gaze isn't so cold. In fact, it feels as if he's seeing me for the first time. My skin heats under his intense scrutiny.

"Are you not wearing pants?" he asks, bringing a hand to the back of his neck.

Shit. I glance down and find that I am, in fact, not wearing pants. "I didn't know you'd be here," I rush out, crossing my legs and tugging at the front of my oversized T-shirt. The move makes the back rise, so I set my tea on the table and hold both sides, then I waddle sideways all the way to my room. "I'm just going to get changed."

Ford stands up and shakes his head, smoothing out the front of his pants again. "No, it's your hotel room. I'll get out of your way. Mel can't get here till tomorrow, but I can be back in an hour. Will you be all right till then?"

"Mel?"

"Melina," he says slowly. "Your best friend, right?"

I tug on the hem of my shirt a little harder and nod. "Yes, she's my best friend. But why is she coming here?"

Oh God, are they replacing me on my own tour? With my best friend? Mel has just as many fans as I do. In fact, I'd say the majority of my fans also love her. And she puts on a great show without all the drama that follows me.

Ford sighs, and his shoulders sag. "Figured we could announce that she'll be joining you for the next few dates. That should take some of the heat off the break-up."

For the first time in the last twelve hours or so, I feel a modicum of relief. "That's brilliant."

Ford's face brightens like my compliment actually affects him. "Glad you think so. So I'll just—" He points to the door. It's a little awkward and so unlike Ford Hall. It's kind of adorable.

"Right. Yes. You go. I'll be here," I say, waddling toward my room again, "not doing crazy things like dancing on bars or walking around without pants in front of my boyfriend's father."

"*Ex*," he growls.

I stumble a bit and have to let go of my shirt with one hand to gain my balance. "Right. Yes. Excellent. Ex-boyfriend. Let's make that clear." With that, I spin, tug on the back of my T-shirt, and rush into the bedroom, praying Ford and I can both forget the last fifteen minutes ever happened.

FORD

4

SNOW ON THE BEACH

This is a bad fucking idea. Even so, I'm standing outside Lake's door, as promised, an hour and a half after leaving her.

Stopping at my apartment in Boston was a necessity. And not only because I needed to shower. No, I had to get the fuck out of there and into my own space, because from the minute I realized Lake wasn't wearing pants, I was sporting a massive hard-on. The last thing that girl needs is to see her ex-boyfriend's father with a woody.

I'm like a prepubescent teen, forgetting proper social etiquette and lusting over a woman almost half my age. Fuck, she's the same age as my children.

It's just wrong.

Not to mention the conflict of interest. I own the label that produces her music.

The lights are flashing red, the gate has been dropped, and the sirens are blaring, but I'm still driving forward like a damn freight train isn't about to take me out.

It's pure idiocy.

I knock and listen for footsteps, all while telling myself that I'm doing the right thing. I own the record label, so it's my job to make sure Lake is in a good place for the tour. And as Paul's father, I need to make sure she's okay.

It's complete and utter bullshit, but when she opens the door and a look of shock mixed with perhaps joy at my arrival crosses her face, I stifle my moral compass. "Ford!" she yelps in what sounds like pleasure as pink travels from her chest to her cheeks, just like my goddamn gaze.

And my dick's hard again.

I'm so fucking screwed.

I let out a surprised laugh at the joy in her tone. "That's me. Can I come in?"

With her lips pressed together, she nods and backs herself against the door, motioning inside. Her hair is wet, like she just got out of the shower, and it's tied back in a ponytail. An oversized black shirt hangs off one shoulder, exposing a bright pink lace strap. Her face is devoid of makeup, and she's no longer pantless. It's wrong, I know, but I'm hit with a bolt of disappointment at the sight of her hot pink leggings. Though it dissipates a bit when I get a good look at the fabric which clings to her legs in a way that should probably be illegal, reminding me of precisely how goddamn perfect she looked this morning.

"You came back," she says softly as she plops onto the couch and pulls her legs beneath her.

My heart sinks a little at the statement. "I told you I would. Did you have plans?" I motion to the door. "I can get out of your way if you want."

"No. I just—" She sighs. "I'm surprised is all. I figured that you'd send someone to check on me. I told you I wouldn't do anything else crazy. I don't need a babysitter."

Ignoring the fact that I may be the one who needs babysitting, I settle next to her on the couch and point to the television. "Figured we could watch a movie and order room service. With the kids at their mother's, I don't have much to do this week. I thought maybe you'd like the company."

Lake's dark brows knit low on her forehead as she studies me. "You want to watch a movie with me?"

Without giving her an answer, I pick up the remote. "How does *Serendipity* sound? Looks like it's available on demand."

The confusion dissipates from Lake's face as a pretty smile takes over. "That's my favorite movie."

"I know." I turn on the TV and navigate to the on-demand options.

Instantly, the pinched brows are back. "How?"

"Ninety-eight percent of the world knows. You've mentioned it in like five interviews." I click on the movie's icon before she can ask me any more questions. I'm not sure I have sufficient answers for the majority of them. Or at least not answers I'm willing to share.

Both of our phones light up intermittently during the movie. I try not to get too distracted, but I can't completely ignore the outside world. Paul has been handled. My other kids, as I told Lake, are busy with their mother. And Lisa has the media covered. My job today is to keep Lake out of the public eye until her show tomorrow night. Once her best friend is here, that job will be significantly easier.

We've leaked a couple of hints about a special guest appearance during her last three shows of this year, and after her show on December thirtieth, she has a two-week break. By the time she performs in Los Angeles, Paul's antics and Lake's reaction will be old news. She'll return home and get back to her job. We just need to make it through the next few shows.

"Oh my God, I would kill for one of those sundaes," Lake groans as John Cusack and Kate Beckinsale devour delicious-looking frozen hot chocolate.

"Ever been?" I ask, hitting Pause on the remote.

"To the restaurant?"

"Yeah. It's your favorite movie. Surely some guy has been smart enough to take you."

Lake stares at me like I have two heads. "I haven't dated a single guy who had the first clue what my favorite movie is, let alone bothered to plan that epic of a date."

"Idiots," I mutter, scrubbing my hand over my face. "You've dated nothing but idiots."

She laughs. "Yeah, it's kind of my MO."

My phone beeps again, and I wince at the name displayed on the screen. Lake's father. He's rightfully pissed. Lake's phone goes off too. She unlocks it and types furiously before tossing it like she wishes she could chuck it out the window.

Immediately, my hackles go up. I don't like seeing her upset. "Someone bothering you?"

She blows out a breath and examines her hands, which are folded together in her lap. "Not the someone who should be bothering me." She peeks up at me. "I know I shouldn't want him to be blowing up my phone, but what does it tell you that I dated your son for two years and he hasn't so much as called to apologize?" The second she finishes the question, she slumps against the couch cushions and turns away again, probably embarrassed.

She has absolutely nothing to feel embarrassed about. It's my son who should be. He's the one who didn't see what a goddamn treasure he had right in front of him; beside him; fuck, even beneath him.

Just the idea of them together makes me feel a rage that is unacceptable. It's the same anger that hit me the first time he brought her to dinner at my home.

He doesn't deserve her. She belongs with someone like me.

Yeah. Those were my first thoughts when he called her his girlfriend. In that moment, I knew I was fucked.

"I forbade him from contacting you."

She side-eyes me, wearing an apprehensive frown. I don't elaborate. The admission is meant to ease her pain. I made the demand, and he didn't fight me on it. An utter disappointment that somehow comforts me now.

"He won't be bothering you," I promise.

Lake worries her lip, but when she nods and her tense shoulders ease, I feel like I've accomplished something today.

My phone rings on the cushion beside me, and this time, I pick up. I need this call to clear my head. I can't be looking at my son's ex this way. Can't reach out to touch her, to comfort her, even if my arms feel empty and my hands itch to do just that.

"Hey, Gav." I stand and head to the floor-to-ceiling windows.

"Coming out tonight?"

I look back at Lake. She's chewing on her finger, zoned out on the movie we left paused on the screen, lost in thought. She's got her legs, still clad in hot pink, pulled up to her chest now, and her long brown hair is escaping her loose ponytail. I spin back and survey the skyline, fisting my free hand to keep from going to her, pushing her hair back behind her ear, and taking her right here on the couch.

She'd probably let me.

What a sick thought.

"Can't, sorry."

"Ah, still cleaning up last night's mess?"

My stomach turns because that's what I should be doing. Not adding to it. "Something like that. Good luck this weekend."

Gavin chuckles. "We wouldn't need luck if you'd let your son play with us now."

"He's finishing college." I shouldn't have to say it. He knows my reasoning.

"Fine, fine. But next year…"

"Next year, he'll get you the cup."

Gavin hisses. "Don't fucking jinx us."

"Please, like you aren't thinking the same thing." I hang up to his laughter and take in the scenery for another moment. The sky is mostly gray. Status quo for Boston in winter. Windows fogged over from the cold. Bare trees. Dirty slush along the roadsides and piled up in parking lots.

In contrast, the warmth in this room is almost stifling. Every bit of the heat is because of the woman behind me. The one I'm trying desperately to ignore.

"If you have to go, it's okay," she says quietly, pulling me from my thoughts.

I don't turn around when I reply. "Actually, I have an idea."

"Oh yeah?" Her tone is immediately lighter.

If I had the balls to turn around, I'd probably see a matching expression on her face. But I need another minute before I do that. I press my hand to the wall and hang my head, trying to get my shit together before I say fuck it and do something I'm sure she'll slap me for.

With a deep inhale, I turn around. "What do you think about taking a ride?"

Lake's responding smile is a shy one. One the world never sees. But she's got her feet firmly planted on the ground and her shoulders back. "Where are we going?"

Unable to help myself, I smile. "That's a surprise. Put on something warm, though. I'll call downstairs and have the valet bring the car around."

When she pulls the red scarf from her bag as we're stepping through the front doors of the hotel, I want to put my fist through the glass.

As if reading my thoughts, she drops her chin and mutters, "Don't have much need for scarves in LA. This is the only one I had."

I shake my head and can't help but give her a sardonic smile. "Need a hat? I've got a matching one."

She coughs out a laugh as I brush past the valet holding open the passenger door. "You noticed that, huh?"

"You're driving," I tell her as I round the car and open the driver's side for her.

She pauses with one hand on the doorframe on the passenger side and eyes me over the roof. "What?"

"You can drive, right?" I shoot her a smirk.

Her face lights up. "No one lets me drive."

With a laugh, I point to the wheel. "Then you better get in before I change my mind."

She squeals and does a little dance on the sidewalk, then mutters an *excuse me* to the valet as she rounds the car. I can't help but laugh. The girl is so fucking polite, so perfect, so goddamn sweet. As she brushes past me, her shoulder skimming against my arm, her sugary scent engulfs me, and I find myself leaning in for another hit. I'm frozen to the spot, watching her as she gets cozy in the driver's seat.

Once she's situated, she looks up at me and grins. "Ready, Daddy Ford?"

Groaning, I knock on the roof of the car and shut the door.

As soon as I'm settled, her questions start again. "Which way?"

"Already set the GPS." I tap on the screen and hit Start, then let the woman's voice direct Lake through traffic. I keep my mouth shut as she winds her way to the interstate and let her focus since she's a little trigger-happy when it comes to the brake. It's a lot of *oh shoots*, *sorry about thats*, and *that car came out of nowhere* comments.

But once we're on the highway and the road opens up, I allow myself to sit back and relax.

"Who called you just before you suggested this trip?" Lake asks.

"Gavin Langfield. He owns the Boston Bolts."

"Right." She nods, not taking her eyes off the road. "Paul mentioned they drafted Daniel. Is he excited?"

I clear my throat. "Yeah, if it was up to him, he'd already be playing."

With a shrug, she dons a soft smile. "It's good that he has to finish college first. I wish my parents had upheld that same kind of rule."

Surprised, I sit forward a little and shift so I'm looking at her profile. "Really?"

"Yeah. I probably wouldn't have listened, but standing on this side of things, I see the benefit. If there comes a day that I can't perform, I have nothing to fall back on."

"Lake, you wouldn't have to work another day in your life if you didn't want to."

She shrugs. "I like working. Even if there comes a day that I don't write music, I can't imagine doing nothing."

"Same."

"Did you always want to do this?"

Cocking my brow, I give her a teasing grin. "Own a label?"

Her responding laugh is breathy. "You know what I mean. Work in music."

Relaxing in my seat, I take a minute to consider her question. "I never made the conscious decision. Music has just always been a part of me."

"You play?"

I huff out a laugh. "Guitar, but not very well."

She glances at me, offering me one of her sweet smiles again. "I could help."

"Ah yes, because you have so much free time. What about you? You always wanted to do this?"

The sigh Lake lets out is a weary one. "I'm sure you've heard me tell my story during a hundred interviews."

"That was Lake the musician. I want you. Not the filtered version. Tell me something about you that Lake Paige would never say in an interview."

For a long moment, she doesn't say anything. She exits the highway when the GPS prompts her to, and when she comes to a stop sign, she grips the wheel tight and swallows thickly. Finally, blue eyes meet mine across the car, and in the moonlight, she glows. "I don't like sex."

"Seriously?" I cough out a surprised laugh. That was the *last* thing I expected to hear come out of her mouth.

She slaps a hand over her face and lowers her head. "Ermygod, I can't believe I just said that."

I'm still in shock, but the words swirl around in my mind, making my blood heat, stirring up feelings I've already fought off once today. "Eyes on me," I grind out.

Obediently, she drops her hands. Her cheeks are tinged pink and her shoulders are slumped, but she doesn't look away. Fuck me, her compliance is too much of a turn-on.

"Seriously, you don't like sex?"

With her lip pulled between her teeth, she shakes her head. "Why would I? It always feels like a lot of work or like I'm not really there. I'm nothing but a prop. It's another performance. I've never felt that connection I sing about. The moment when two people become one. The heat, the passion, the..." She falters, pulling back a fraction.

I keep my eyes on her, silently imploring her to finish. Damn if she doesn't have my heart beating out of my chest.

"The love," she finally says. "I've never felt that. So yeah, I just don't get the big deal surrounding it."

She turns away from me, and when traffic clears, she turns onto the road that leads to the beach.

Once parked, she stares out the windshield silently, her hands still on the wheel and her shoulders practically touching her ears.

With irritation simmering just below my skin, I get out of the car, round it, and throw open her door. "Goddamn idiots."

"Hmm?" she says, looking up at me with wide eyes, as if she's just realized I'm still here.

"The men you've dated. Every one of them. Now come on. Let's get some fresh air and forget about them."

"We're walking on the beach?" she questions, though she slides her palm into mine and allows me to lead her down to the sand.

The ocean is reckless in front of us, thrashing and angry as it rolls up onto the shore. I've never related to a body of water more.

"Yes." It's a fight to keep my grip loose on her hand when I come to a stop and turn to her. I want to squeeze it tight and pull her close. "I'm going to show you how a real man would treat you."

With that damn red lip between her teeth again, she tilts her head up to look me right in the eye. As she does, a single snowflake lands on the tip of her nose. A delighted squeal falls from her lips. "Oh!"

Fat flakes fall from the sky after that, one after another. Lake lets go of my hand and spins with her head tipped back and her arms outstretched. "It's snowing," she whispers, like the magic will stop if she draws too much attention to it.

Right now, though? She's the magic. The way she moves, so care-free. Not worrying who will see her or what they'll think leaves her reactions effortless.

Just as we can't pocket the snowflakes because they'll melt the instant we touch them, I know I'm not supposed to touch her. But fuck, that doesn't stop her from grabbing for the snowflakes, and suddenly I find myself reaching for her. I pull her against my chest, stealing her magic for just a few seconds.

"It's beautiful," she whispers, her breath unsteady as she looks up at me.

"Most beautiful thing I've ever seen," I murmur back, my mouth far too close to hers.

I think we both know it's not the snow I'm talking about.

LAKE
5

I KNEW YOU WERE TROUBLE.

ord Hall's lips are millimeters from mine. He's going to kiss me.
A full-body shiver runs through me at just the thought, but Ford
misinterprets the response and frowns.

"You're freezing. Let's get you back into the car."

My stomach sinks, and a blast of cold air hits me as he backs away
and drops the hold he has on me. A moment later, he wraps one arm
around my shoulder and guides me to the car. This hold is different.
Like a caretaker, like he's minding me. Keeping his most talented
client safe. I want to protest. This is the first time I've been truly alone
with someone in…God, I don't even know how long.

I'm constantly being watched, photographed. Fans are always
close, waiting for a signature or a moment of my attention. But not
today. Ford watched my favorite movie with me, he let me drive his
car, and he brought me to the beach so I could have a little time by
myself.

He gave me quiet.

And now all I want are his words. I want to know what he's thinking. About me. This situation. About my confession about hating sex.

God, what a stupid thing to say.

"Want to drive?" he asks as we reach the car.

I shake my head, unable to make words work.

Like a gentleman, Ford opens my door, and after I climb in, he tugs at the seat belt, leans across me, and buckles me in. That damn masculine scent surrounds me again, and I have to clutch my knees to keep from reaching for him. He pulls back, but only a few inches, and tilts his face toward mine. When he moves in again, he brushes my hair behind my ear. The move is so small, so simple, but it steals all the air from my lungs. He closes his eyes, and I study his face up close. His dark lashes against his cheekbones, the faint creases around his eyes. For several heartbeats, he doesn't let go of my cheek.

My heart beats out a rhythm on my breastbone, one wholly made up of desire and longing. I close my eyes and soak in the feeling, readying myself for the moment he leans in. The hunger raging inside me is quickly replaced with a flooding disappointment, though, when his hand drops from my skin and the door closes.

"Get a grip," I whisper to myself, rubbing my palms against my thighs as I watch him round the hood.

As the car rumbles to life, his warm palm lands on my hand, and when I turn it so that I can hold his, he waffles our fingers together.

And that's how we drive all the way back to the hotel. No words. No questions. Just silence and his hand in mine.

When we pull up to the hotel, Ford rasps, "I'll walk you up." He finally lets go of my hand and climbs out of the car. The loss of him is acute. In the course of just a few hours, things between us have shifted in a monumental way. We're on the precipice of the unknown, and I think we both know that the moment we're in my suite, there won't be any going back.

The need to feel his hands on my body consumes my every thought, leaving no room to second guess the bad decision I'm dying to make. For the first time in years, I couldn't give a shit about anything but what I want. Not Paul. Not the repercussions. Not the implications surrounding my desire to fuck his dad.

No, I'm consumed with nothing but Ford and the way he made me feel today.

Seen. Desired. Respected. Treasured.

Sex with him? There's no way it could be boring. He's so present, so attentive. I can't imagine he'd ever treat his partner like a prop. No, sex with Ford Hall would be impossibly memorable. He'd worship every inch of me. Might actually snap me in two. The man is huge.

When he opens the door and holds out his hand to me, I dip my chin and take it, snuggling in close to him, allowing his tall frame to hide me from any prying eyes. As we enter the hotel, I'm ready to devour him. We've almost made it to the elevator when I hear my name.

"Lake!"

Ford's arm tightens around me, acting as my shield, but the voice is so familiar and so welcome that I can't help but turn toward it. She's already barreling toward us, loudly and unapologetically, so I take a step to the side and brush off his arm.

"Melina." I throw out my arms to her. "You're here."

Beside me, Ford steps back and straightens. The desire in his gaze evaporates, and he settles back into his record label owner persona. *Our* record label owner.

"Daddy Ford, you did good! My girl looks so much better than I expected," Mel says as she spins, taking me with her so we're both facing him.

"I did nothing." He lifts his chin, steady, professional. "Just happy you're here to take over."

Ouch.

The words are like a sucker punch, the meaning behind them nearly knocking me over. He was just doing his job. Keeping his most profitable artist content and out of trouble. Now my best friend is here to take over—she'll take care of poor Lake. The girl who clearly can't take care of herself. The one who's always falling for the wrong man.

The girl who mistakes simple kindness for something else completely.

Shame washes over me, and I let out a breathy sob of a laugh. "No need, I'm good. Let's head up to the room. Don't want any more debacles with the press." Without looking up, I bite out, "Don't worry, Mr. Hall, we'll be good."

"Right," he says, his voice sharp. "Have a good night, ladies. I'll see you tomorrow at the stadium."

Mel doesn't even wait for him to move out of earshot before she's whispering in my ear, "Oh, Daddy Ford is looking *migh-ty* fine. Wouldn't mind working out my daddy issues with him."

"Oh my God," I hiss. Heart lodged in my throat, I peek back, but he's already stepping out the front doors. I wasn't even worth a second look.

"What?" she whines, tugging on my arm.

For the first time since I've seen her, I actually *see* her. Her blond hair is styled perfectly, and she's wearing black leather pants, a slouchy gray sweater, and spiked heels. She is clearly dressed to be seen.

I drag her in the direction of the elevator because I have no intention of being seen anywhere, but she pulls me back.

"We are so not going to bed right now. You need a revenge fuck. You need to dance all over this city and make out with every hot man you see."

"*Daddy Ford*," I say with a bit of bite, "will kill us if we go out."

"I'd gladly take the punishment." She sticks her ass out and taps it. "Oh, Daddy, I'm so sorry I've been a bad girl."

I yank her as hard as I can toward the elevator, praying that no one caught that on film. Girl is on a roll. There is no way we're leaving my hotel room.

The next three days are a whirlwind of work. Before every show, Mel swears she's going to force me to go out, but fortunately, even she's too tired after dancing on stage for hours between rehearsal and the actual concerts to push too hard.

On New Year's Eve—having still not heard a word from Paul—I'm over licking my wounds. It's ridiculous how little his disappearance has affected my life. How nothing about my day-to-day has changed. Well, other than not having to coddle someone who didn't give two shits about me.

We're rehearsing for a last-minute private show for the Bolts, and I'm sweating up a storm when Ford walks in flanked by two men in expensive suits. A black Henley pulls against his muscles as he lets out a loud laugh.

My heart takes off at a gallop at the sound, threatening to launch right out of my chest. God, the man has a beautiful laugh.

The men on either side of him are equally gorgeous. I swear one is the spitting image of Henry Cavill, with green eyes and a bit of a frown, and the other looks like Bradley Cooper. He's wearing a smirk, like he's quite proud of his ability to make Ford laugh so brazenly.

Mel nudges me so hard I stumble. "Now that's a gang bang I'd sign up for."

The bark of laughter that escapes me practically echoes in the space before I can clap a hand over my mouth. I don't catch myself quickly enough, and now all three men are surveying me.

Ford steps closer. "Something funny?" His eyes dance like he knows exactly what we're giggling about.

As if I wasn't hot enough already, his attention ramps up the temperature in the room. I pull my hair off my neck and hold it up as I attempt to come up with a reply.

Ford tilts his head to one side and frowns, then he slides something off his wrist and holds it out to me. "You're always forgetting these."

Because I'm a people pleaser, I reach for the object he's handing me without thought. A hair elastic? I hold it between my fingers like it might slither at me, dumbfounded by the gesture.

"Need me to put it in your hair too?" he teases.

The room is dead silent, and I'm pretty sure every eye is trained on us. Did Ford just pull a scrunchie off his wrist and give it to me?

"Um, no." Quickly, I use it to pull my hair back in a sloppy pony-tail. "Thanks."

He's right, I am always forgetting them. My hair drives me crazy when it's loose like this during rehearsal. Before every show, my stylist applies so much product it barely moves while I'm on stage, but if we set it too early, it won't hold until the end of the night. But the elastics dig into my wrists, so I never have one handy.

Ford shrugs like it's no big deal despite the fact that we're all gaping at him. "Ready for tonight, ladies?"

Mel's phone buzzes on the table, pulling her from the conversation.

"Yeah," I say. "I think we're set. Hopefully the guys paying for the private show are happy."

The Bradley Cooper look-alike nods. "Very happy. We appreciate your willingness to do this at the last minute." He holds out his hand. "I'm Gavin, and this is my brother Beckett. We own the team."

I suck in a breath and perk up. "Oh! You're Ford's friends."

In unison, the brothers side-eye Ford, like they're surprised I know this. It's only because he told me about them in the car. Nothing else nefarious. Hell, since that odd moment on the beach where I thought he wanted to kiss me, he's been basically MIA.

Though not so MIA that he missed the way I always forget hair ties. And if the chai tea and chocolate milk delivered daily are any indication, he's still thinking about me.

"That motherfucker," Mel growls from the floor where she's leaned against the wall, her phone in hand. She tips her head back and sneers at Ford. "Your fucking son. Why the fuck would you let him do this?"

My lungs practically seize as I look from her to Ford and back again. I'm not sure anyone has ever spoken to him this way. Certainly not one of his musicians. What the hell did Paul do now?

His only reaction is a tick of his jaw.

Beside him, Gavin has his phone out and his head tipped low. After a moment, he hands Ford his phone. And that's when I see an image of my ex-boyfriend and his new boyfriend clad in swim trunks and nothing else, making out on the beach.

Ford curses and shakes his head, and then he's pulling out his own phone and growling into it.

When Mel approaches me, sympathy in her expression, rage like I've never known flows through my blood. Paul is nothing but trouble. She squeezes my hand, but I shake her off.

"I think I'm ready for that revenge now."

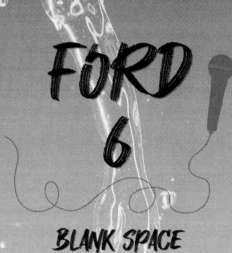

FORD
6

BLANK SPACE

"I told you this wasn't a fucking vacation," I growl, propping myself up against the wall in the owner's suite at the arena.

I'm shocked that Paul actually had the balls to pick up the phone. Then again, he's sporting an extra pair these days now that he has his boyfriend by his side. What the fuck?

"Listen, Dad, I know you don't like the media circus, but I'm happy. Why can't you just be happy for me?"

Closing my eyes and letting out a breath, I drop my head back against the wall. What the fuck am I supposed to say to that? I could give two fucks who my son dates. And of course I want him to be happy. But what he's doing is cruel. Parading around and flaunting his new relationship after cheating on Lake. Knowing she'll see it all. My anger has nothing to do with who he's dating and everything to do with how he's gone about this entire thing.

"How are you paying for a vacation in Bali?"

Paul practically chokes on his words. "My credit card, obviously."

Flames erupt inside me.

Obviously. This fucking kid.

I pinch the bridge of my nose. "You don't have a job, Paul. And you don't understand the first thing about responsibility. You fucked up, and rather than owning it and doing what I asked so that you wouldn't hurt Lake even more than you already have, you're fucking gallivanting around on *my* dime. It ends now. I'm shutting off your card access. Hope it was worth it."

Without waiting for a response, I tap End and throw my phone onto the couch.

"How can we help?" Gavin asks, hauling himself up from one of the seats behind the glass. The private show for the players is set to begin in thirty minutes, and I can't imagine what's going through Lake's mind.

"He was supposed to go to my cabin in the mountains. Lay low for a few weeks. Let the girl lick her wounds. He couldn't even give her that." I shake my head. He's so fucking clueless.

Beckett pulls on his neck. "She seemed okay when she walked off."

I roll my eyes. He has no idea what a woman needs. The man still can't admit to himself that he's obsessed with his head of PR. And she's completely unavailable. It's ridiculous.

So excuse me for not taking his word for it. I need to make sure Lake's fine myself. With a huff, I pocket my phone and turn on my heel.

Gavin grabs for me as I head toward the door. "Give her some space. She mentioned revenge. Sounds to me like she needs to find a guy to fuck. Ya know, move on from the humiliation and feel wanted again."

The fire inside me flashes hotter at the image of Lake wrapped around a faceless man. "That's the last thing she needs," I grit out through clenched teeth.

"Respectfully," Gavin holds up a hand, "it's not up to you to figure out what she needs. She's your son's ex."

Both brothers blink at me like I've lost my damn mind. Maybe I have, because I stopped thinking of Lake as my son's anything the moment she looked at me like she wanted me to kiss her. And if I'm honest, I probably haven't considered her his for a lot longer than that.

But because she is, in fact, *his* ex, I stalk to the bar rather than the door, and pour myself a ginormous glass of whiskey.

LAKE
7

DRESS

"This look okay?" I spin in the mirror and tug at the hem of the sparkly rose gold number that hits high on my thigh. I'm pretty sure I've got more skin on display than what's covered under this thing, but it's New Year's Eve. Isn't that what tonight is for?

Short dresses, flirty smiles, bad decisions.

Hmm, sounds like a good song.

"You look like porn on a stick," Mel says with a shimmy of her hips.

"I have no idea what that means." But I giggle anyway.

Mel hovers close behind me and squeezes my shoulder. "Proud of you," she says, locking eyes with me in the mirror.

Our show went off without a hitch, and then Ford's friends invited us to a swanky private party.

"Hockey players in suits," Mel crooned on our way back to the suite to get ready. "My lady bits are going to have so much fun tonight!"

With a swipe of my signature red lipstick, I smile. "Operation Revenge is in full swing."

"Oh yes! We should take a pic and post it. Show Paul you're moving on."

"Eh, fuck him, honestly. Tonight is for me. I'm getting revenge on myself. I'm tired of being the woman who gets walked on."

"No, you're getting revenge on them. On all the men who were stupid enough to take you for granted. We're gonna dance on their graves!"

That doesn't sound quite right, but she's just crazy enough that it makes sense.

IT'S BEEN years since I had the ability to blend in with the crowd. Throw Mel into the mix, and there's no point in trying. But an event like this is the exception. Hockey players are used to attention, often having women throw themselves at them and grown men beg for their signatures, so the majority of them don't bombard us. With the exception of the younger guys and their dates. They're still a bit green.

We've only made it two steps toward the bar when the first guy offers to buy us a drink.

Mel looks him up and down appreciatively and nods. He's tall, not shocking, muscular, also not shocking, and sporting a black eye.

"Looks like he can handle himself," Mel chirps as he guides us to the bar.

"Or maybe he walked into a coat rack?" I tease.

She rolls her eyes. "Don't ruin it for me."

"What would you like?" Mr. Tall, Muscular, and Battered asks us.

Over his shoulder, I spot Ford. He's at the other end of the bar, and he's changed out of the Henley from earlier. Now he's decked out in a black suit that tugs across his back and leaves his ass looking biteable. Yes, every man in this room has an incredible body, but they're all boys in comparison to him. The way he carries himself, his cool confidence, makes it tempting to reply to this guy with something like *"Him. That's what I like."* Of course, I'd never be so bold. So instead, I say, "A vodka soda, please."

When we've got our drinks in hand, our new friend diverts all his attention to Mel again. Not that I blame him since my focus is not up for grabs. Ford Hall commands every ounce of it. As I take a sip and search for an excuse to approach him, another woman beats me to it.

Lisa. His number two.

She's got long red hair, beautiful violet eyes, and a beauty mark above her lip that is fucking tantalizing.

She's drop-dead gorgeous, with amazing curves and a set of tits that have every person she passes noticing. She looks like Jessica Rabbit, and from the looks of things, she's set her sights on Ford.

A twinge of jealousy so acute I can't help but rub at it settles itself between my ribs. The pain blossoms into a stabbing sensation when she grips Ford's arm and leans in to whisper in his ear.

When he drops his head back and laughs, I bite my lip to hold back my groan of annoyance.

I shouldn't be looking at my ex's father this way.

I shouldn't be looking at the head of my label this way.

For my entire life, I've done the right thing. Not once have I let myself think about a person in a position of power the way I am now. Not because I think he'd take advantage of me. But because people would assume I got where I am by sleeping with a man like him.

I didn't work this hard to give the world even an inkling of doubt about how I got here.

But God, when his eyes cut in my direction and his entire demeanor shifts, like he's stunned to see me, my damn heart flutters right out of my chest.

Maybe I shouldn't give a damn what people think.

Jessica—a.k.a. Lisa, a.k.a. the bane of my existence—tugs on Ford's jacket and takes a step closer. He watches me for one more beat, though he doesn't acknowledge me with even a nod or a smile. Then he's tearing his gaze back toward the bar.

And away from me.

"Want a shot?" Mel pushes one forward without waiting for my reply.

Without hesitation, I toss the golden liquid back and slam the shot glass onto the bar. And when another hockey player approaches and asks if I want to dance, I also don't hesitate.

"I'm Camden," he says as he leads me toward the space where bodies are grinding against one another.

With the lights dimmed, the city sparkles through the expansive windows. On the other side of the dance floor, a DJ dances along with the upbeat music he's mixing.

"Lake," I reply.

The blond chuckles. "Yes, I'm aware."

His palm finds my lower back, and he presses me close as soon as we hit the dance floor. The man doesn't exude an ounce of shyness as he grinds against me.

One song turns into two, and before the third begins, Mel appears with another shot and a fresh vodka soda. For the first time in I don't know how long, I lose myself in my surroundings. I feel like I'm part of something. I'm entertained, rather than being the entertainment.

Hot and in need of a break, Mel and I promise we'll return, then sneak off to the bar, positioning ourselves outside the fray.

"You going to test drive that hockey player's stick?" Mel wiggles her shoulders and smiles.

With a lift of one shoulder, I check out Camden, who's also stepped off the dance floor and is chatting with a few other players. "Maybe. I mean, why not?" For once I'm not worrying about the consequences. Tonight is about having fun.

Mel jumps in place and grasps my forearm. "Gotta pee. You want to come?"

I shake my head. "It's almost midnight. Don't be gone too long."

"Oh, please. You'll be sucking face with lover boy over there by the time I come back." She points to Camden, who is now walking toward me, all swagger and sex.

Tucking a strand of hair behind my ear, I spin to the bar and order another drink. I'm not ready for good ole sex eyes yet. On the opposite end of the bar, Ford is still standing with his friends. They're surrounded by a few women who keep inching closer. One of them being Lisa.

I always liked her.

Tonight, I want to claw her eyes out.

I'm a glutton for punishment, I guess, because I can't help but peek over at the group again. This time, though, the man I can't stop thinking about meets my eye and holds my attention. I snag the drink the bartender slides across the bar and hold it up in a salute of sorts.

His face breaks out in a surprised smile. "Having fun?" he mouths.

I shoot him a crooked smile and dip my head in affirmation.

He pulls up straighter and shifts his body, like he's about to shoulder past his friends and maybe utter an *excuse me*, but my focus is pulled away from him when an overheated palm lands on my ass.

"Get me one?" Camden murmurs into my ear before nuzzling into my neck. He's sweaty from dancing, though he smells delicious, but my mind is still on Ford. I attempt to shift out of his embrace so that I don't lose sight of the object of my obsession, but when I look up, expecting to see Ford walking toward me, I realize he never moved from his spot.

Disappointment settles like a rock in my stomach. Dammit. Apparently I've developed a rather annoying crush on my ex's father.

I motion to the bartender for Camden, and once we both have our drinks, I lead him back to the dance floor.

Mel appears five minutes before midnight and joins us. We get lost in dancing again. Bodies sway, music taking over. When Camden leans in, it's obvious he's about to kiss me. The idea of his lips against mine feels heavy, like if I let him, it will weigh me down for far longer than just tonight. Avoiding the contact, I spin and grind my ass against him. His hands are everywhere, sliding over my hips, along my ribs, under my breasts. But then I'm pulled forward, out of his grasp.

"What the hell?" he yells.

I blink twice, sure that I'm seeing things. Shocked that the man looming over me is the one I've been desperate for all night.

Ford's jaw is clenched and his hair is mussed like he's been pulling at it. I like to imagine I had something to do with that.

"What are you doing?" I whisper as he grasps my waist with both hands and pulls me closer to him—and farther from Camden's grip.

"Get lost," he says over my head.

I should turn around. I should at least apologize to the man I've spent the last hour dancing with. Flirting with. Letting believe he had a shot.

But I don't.

There's only one person whose attention I've wanted, and now that I have it, I'm not giving up even a second of it.

"I said, what are you doing?" This time my voice is louder, my stare challenging, eyebrow arched, lips pulled together, waiting for him to finally make his damn move.

Ford's thumb ever so gently rubs back and forth against my ass. It's barely noticeable in the dark. Imperceptible really, but the simple caress sets my skin ablaze.

"What are *you* doing?" He crowds me, his head tilted low. His tone is a warning. It's dark and a bit angry, in complete contrast to the way he's holding me. The way he's touching me.

"I was trying to get revenge. Ya know, a little New Year's Eve fun? Maybe fuck someone in public. Show the world that I'm over your son and his cheating ways."

Ford's jaw ticks and his chest heaves so violently it presses against mine with each inhale, but he doesn't say a word. Goading him is probably a bad idea, and I definitely shouldn't say what I'm thinking, but my lips don't seem to get the memo. "If I really want revenge, though, maybe I should just fuck his dad."

FORD

8

DANCING WITH OUR HANDS TIED

I'm rendered speechless, but I have yet to let go of Lake. In fact, my hold on her has gotten tighter. There's no way I'm going to allow her to escape. Allow another man to touch her.

Fuck that.

For the past hour, I've watched her every move. Every sway of her hips on the dance floor. So intently that Gavin and Beckett settled for talking around me. Eventually, they pushed me forward, telling me if I was going to make it this obvious, then I might as well get it over with and take her.

I considered staying put, pushed away the need clawing its way through me, knowing she didn't need the mess. But then that fucker leaned in for a kiss. She's lucky she maneuvered out of his hold the way she did. If I'd had to break up a kiss, I would have done it with my fist, and that asshole would have been laid out in the middle of the crowd.

Fuck, she makes me crazy.

Around us, the countdown begins. Every person chanting.

"Five."

Lake moves closer, if that's possible.

"Four."

She tips her head back, her eyes sparkling brighter than I've ever seen.

"Three."

Her red lips taunt me as she says, "Let me go if you don't want me to kiss you."

"Two."

I don't make a move.

"One. Happy New Year!"

The crowd around us erupts. The music gets louder, and we're being pushed and pulled from every side. Having not taken my eyes off her mouth, when it curves in the tiniest smile, I know she knows I'm not pulling away. She lifts up on her tiptoes, and then her famous red lips are on mine.

The taste of lime and something sweet infiltrates my system, sending a bolt of lust straight through me. I let out a groan as she sweeps her tongue against my own. Her lips are pillowy soft, and she smells so goddamn good. Sugary. Like a fudge shop. Sweet and innocent.

Nothing I deserve.

With one hand on her hip, I pull her closer. I cuff the back of her neck with the other, holding her in place. She melts against me, allowing me to take and take and take.

We need to get out of here.

When I pull away, she whimpers and grasps the lapels of my suit jacket, bringing me closer again. "Please." Those red lips pout.

"I'm not stopping, gorgeous. Just need you alone," I murmur with one more peck to her sinful mouth.

She smiles against me. "My hotel?"

"I've got a room here. Follow me." Another of my friends owns this hotel. I got a room in case I decided to stay, not that I ever imagined the night would end like this.

Then again, I never intended to let her leave with anyone else, so it's unlikely it would have ended in any way but this: with her gripping my arm as I nod to Gavin and weave my way out of the room.

My best friend drops his head between his shoulders to hide the smile that splits his face. I can only imagine his thoughts. Fucking old man going after a hot young thing like her. His son's ex-girlfriend at that. Fuck.

I'm a parody. But I honestly don't give a damn. There's no room for judgment when my mind is filled with all the things I'm going to do to her. The ways I intend to touch her. Lake will finally understand the hype around sex. She'll be begging to suck my cock and ride me after tonight.

As soon as we step into the foyer, away from the music and the chatter of the crowd, we're hit with reality. It's brighter out here, making us more visible to the people who gape as I lead her toward the elevator.

She can't go anywhere without being noticed, gawked at, ogled. It's nothing new, but she tenses beside me at the scrutiny, obviously uncomfortable, so I pull her into my side and wrap my jacket around her, offering her as much anonymity as I can.

"Thank you," she murmurs against my chest, her brown hair a curtain over her beautiful eyes.

As soon as the elevator arrives, I guide her inside, then turn and glare at the man trying to follow us in. "Take the next one." I hit the button for our floor, and as soon as the door closes on the man's scowl, I peer down at the gorgeous woman who's got me acting absolutely insane. "You okay?"

Eyes the color of the sky on the sunniest of days widen as they study me. "You must think I've lost my mind."

"Why?"

"I propositioned you. I kissed you. God, Ford, I'm so sorry." A blush creeps up her cheeks, and she buries her head in my chest.

With a finger under her chin, I gently force her head up until she's looking at me. She's got the smallest cleft right in the center, like it was made for my thumb, so I hold her there as I bring my mouth closer to hers. "Don't apologize for giving me everything I've been thinking about since I first laid eyes on you."

"Tonight?" she murmurs, pulling back a fraction and scanning my face.

A bitter smile forms on my lips as I shake my head and brush my lips to hers. "No. The day you walked into my office and introduced yourself. You were wearing a red tank top with black lettering on it. A black skirt that made my cock jump to attention, and pink nail polish on your toes."

She inhales sharply, and her eyes widen at my confession.

"And these lips. Fuck, Red, you could bring a grown man to his knees with these goddamn lips."

Her pupils blow wide in response, and when I press on her bottom lip, she moans.

"We don't have to do anything you don't want to do, but I'd really like to show you what all the fuss is about."

Lake swipes her tongue across her bottom lip, brushing the tip along my thumb as she does. Her responding sigh is just as breathy as the one that escapes me. Then she does it again, this time inching farther so my thumb slides into her mouth. I hook it there, trapping her, and she moans around it, circling it with her tongue in a teasing way that has me pushing her against the elevator wall. Before we can take it further, though, the door chimes and the stainless-steel doors slide open soundlessly.

"What do you say, Red? You coming?" I tease, backing away with one hand extended to her.

Lake smirks and settles her hand in mine. "I better be, old man."

With a bark of shocked laughter, I grasp her around the middle and throw her over my shoulder. With a slap to her ass, I head toward my room. "I'll show you how old I am. I should put you over my knee and make you beg for it."

She giggles as she bounces on my shoulder. The movement and the hallway lights bouncing off her glittery dress highlight her ass, making it impossible not to sink my teeth into it as we go.

"Oh my God, Ford!"

Her reprimands only make my need for her grow. I love the sound of her screams. Love the way she's letting loose. The prim and proper Lake is nowhere to be seen tonight. And I intend to fuck the proper right out of her for good.

I breeze into my room and toss her onto the bed, loving the look of shock that mars her pretty face as she gapes up at me. Her body arches on instinct as she props herself up on her elbows. Her legs are sprawled out on the duvet, like she's a doll just begging to be played with. She opens her mouth, maybe to try to rationalize what's happening. That won't do either of us any good, so I drop one knee to the edge of the bed and grab her right foot, pulling her closer. Then I climb over her and pin her beneath me.

"I'm going to kiss you now."

She smiles as I make my descent, and then our lips are mashing together. This isn't gentle. No, I'm fucking her with my mouth. Devouring her. Eating up her little sounds. Tasting her every caress. Her moans are fuel to the fire in my blood, scorching every inch of me and leaving a trail of nothing but her.

With just one kiss, she's destroyed me. Owned me. Changed me on a cellular level—from the man I was minutes ago to the man I am now. *Hers.*

It's only fair I return the favor. "Now tell me, Red, do you like touching yourself, or is that also overrated?"

Lake turns her head, her pretty blue eyes finding the window, avoiding my scrutiny.

I press my thumb to the space in her chin made just for it and force her to look at me. "Don't get shy now, gorgeous. You wanted to fuck your ex's dad. *You* stole the kiss. Tonight is all about you. Tell me what you like."

She squirms beneath me, bucking up to seek more of the friction we created with our previous indelicate kisses.

"Do you want me to kiss you here?" I press my lips to her collarbone and enjoy the shivers that skate across her skin in response. "Or here?" This time, I brush my lips across her chest, dragging my tongue against her sweet skin as I do. "Or here?" I nip at the swell of her breast, then suck on it, surely leaving a mark. I intend to mark her entire body.

She throws her head back and groans.

Her dress is a distraction. The sequins catch the light of the moon, casting her in an angelic glow. I don't want her to look like an angel tonight. She's sin, a temptress with her red lips and rocking hips, her legs around my waist and her ankles locked at the small of my back as she tries to get me closer.

A dark chuckle escapes me, sending goose bumps rippling across the skin of her neck. "For someone who doesn't like sex, you're awfully greedy for it."

"Why do I have the feeling you're about to destroy every misconception I've ever had?" she whispers, arching up and grinding against me, trying like hell to ride my cock.

I cage her in so she can't look away from me and pin her with a pointed look. "Because I am. I'm going to obliterate you, Red. Going to make you beg for every orgasm. You'll be my dirty slut. You won't say please and you won't say thank you. You'll take it all. You'll ride me hard and ensure that the only one grateful here is me. Because I'll know that I made you this way."

"Oh fuck." She slaps the mattress on either side of her. "Why is that so hot?" Her whimpers get louder as I slide a hand beneath her dress and give her nipple a hard pluck.

"Because you're a slut and you've been waiting for this. Because your pussy needs this. It's not your fault you've never been satisfied, Red. You've never had a man who took the time to worship you. Now turn over so I can unzip this dress and see every inch of skin you've been hiding from me."

She complies without a word. I hate it and love it at the same time. I want her to take control. I want her to be free of the compulsion to perform. For once, I want her to be the Lake who doesn't overthink what she's doing.

But maybe that's exactly who she is right now. Maybe she doesn't have to think too hard about this because what we're doing is innate. Natural. There are thousands of critics out there who wouldn't believe it, but having Lake beneath me feels more natural than anything I've ever experienced.

More explosive too.

This girl is going to blow up my world, and I'm going to stand back and let her.

I press a kiss to the base of her neck, then lick a path downward, tracing the arch of her back with my tongue until I reach the top of her dress. Without pulling my lips away, I grasp the zipper and ease it lower, then follow its trail with my mouth, baring her smooth skin to the moonlight. Fuck, if I thought her dress sparkled, it has nothing on her.

She's an angel on earth, and I'm about to drag her toward the fires of hell.

With one hand, I undo the clasp of her bra and then follow the arc of her ribs until I can cup the swell of her breast in my hand. "You're perfect," I murmur against her neck.

She bucks her ass against me, forcing a puff of air from my lungs.

"So greedy. Don't worry, Red. I'm getting there."

"Get there faster," she grinds out, finally demanding what she wants.

I peel the straps down both of her arms until I'm sliding off the bed and taking the dress with me. She's left in nothing but a scrap of red lace between her ass cheeks and black stilettos with red soles that sway as she shimmies her hips, putting on a little show.

With a fist to my mouth, I let out a guttural groan. "Fucking perfection. Now turn over and cup those perfect tits so I can see just how dirty you are."

Instead of listening, she pushes up onto her knees, crosses her ankles, and sticks her ass out. When she looks at me over her shoulder, the liquid heat in her eyes begs me to dive in. She's tantalizing. "Make me."

Grasping her thighs so hard my nails puncture her skin, I pull her so her ass is flush against my hard length. I lift her hips slightly and roll her pussy against my cock, one way, then the other, so she can feel every fucking inch of me beneath my suit. "That's how you want to play it?"

"Yes," she breathes, head dropped between her shoulders. "Treat me like your little whore. Make me come all over your cock."

Holding her up with one hand, I land a sharp slap to her bare ass, pulling a perfect scream from her. Immediately, I rub at the sting. "You gushing for me, Red? Soaking those panties because you love the feel of my hands on your ass?"

"Yes, Daddy." Her moans are hoarse, desperate.

My body goes to war with itself then. The inferno raging inside me isn't all desire when her words register. "Don't you fucking dare," I growl, crashing my hand down on her other cheek.

"You don't like it when your dirty whore calls you Daddy?" she taunts, pressing her ass against my dick and rubbing.

It pisses me the fuck off. Makes my skin itch. I'm not her goddamn daddy. The things I want to do to her? Fuck no.

"I'm your ex's Daddy, Lake. Remember that when you come all over my cock. I'm the one who gets you there. I'm the one you'll be calling for. You'll say my name only when you come. Test it out for me. Say *my* name."

"F-Ford," she whimpers, her legs shaking beneath her as she tries to get closer.

I hold her in place. "Say it like you know you hold all the control, Red. Say it like you own me, because tonight, you do."

Her back rises and falls as she takes a deep breath. Then she pushes up on her hands and looks at me, her blue eyes lit with pure desire. "Then turn me around and fuck me, Ford. No more teasing. Give me *my* fucking cock."

That's my goddamn girl. I flip her over by her ankles in one rough move, and she falls against the bed with a thud. Without taking my eyes off her, I shuck off my jacket and pants, then get to work on the buttons of my shirt.

Her gaze alone is hot enough to set fire to my clothes. She tweaks her nipples and writhes on the bed, then she snakes one hand down her abdomen until it disappears beneath her sin-red panties. With rapt attention, I take in the way she teases her clit, soaking the lace with her arousal.

"Good girl. Make yourself come, Red. I want to taste it."

She thrashes against her hand, working herself harder. Unable to stay away, I drop one hand to the mattress and hold myself above her, pressing my lips to her ankle, then her calf, before I pull her legs wide open and lick up her thigh. Sweet moans fill the air, and with my lips still on the smooth, sensitive skin of her inner leg, I peer up at her and watch as she begins to come apart. My patience sapped, I run my tongue along the seam of her panties, savoring her sweet saltiness, and pull the fabric aside so I can lick a path between her lips. That one pass is all it takes for her to shatter beneath me. I don't pull away. No, I double down on my work, relishing the way her pussy pulses around my tongue as she does exactly as I request.

"Yes, Ford. Fuck yes. That feels amazing."

I suck on her clit and lap at her, making her squirm and beg, just like I promised she would.

"Oh God—"

I halt my movements and chastise her. "What's my name?"

"Ford—" she whimpers. "Ford, please don't stop."

With a dark chuckle, I pull back a fraction. "No manners, Red. Make demands. Take what you want."

Long legs that I've dreamed about far more than I should circle my neck and hold me in place as she thrusts against my face.

"Fuck yes. Fuck my face, gorgeous. Use me to come."

She does just that. She takes all the control and uses my tongue like I'm her toy. Like I'm here solely for her pleasure. It's the hottest fucking thing I've ever experienced. When her movements steady out, I cup her ass with both hands and flip us so I'm on my back and her knees are planted on either side of my head. She picks up again instantly and rides me until she's crying out that she's coming again.

I press soft kisses against her skin as she saws in sharp breaths above me. "I don't think I can take any more."

Her body is glistening from the work she put in to get to her orgasm, her breasts heavy and her blue eyes shining with delight.

"You can and you will," I promise. "Now lay down on that pillow while I get a condom. And take those panties off. I'm going to fuck you now."

She practically squeals as she scampers into position. Fuck, she's cute. I can't help but laugh at the move as I climb off the bed. My cock bobs heavily as I shuffle to where I tossed my pants and dig the condom out of my wallet. I rip it open and enjoy the way she waits for me. Splayed out against the white sheets, her hair a riot around her. Eyes wide and hazy, lips parted as she stares unabashedly.

Headed back to the bed, my cock in hand, I tug the condom over the already dripping tip. "You going to take me like a good girl, Red? Mold yourself around me? *Milk me?*" I tighten my grip around my cock to quell the urge to fuck into her hard.

She nods. "Yes." It's a pant. A plea.

I climb onto the bed and settle myself between her thighs, pulling her knees up so the points of her black heels dig into the mattress. The whimper that leaves her as I slide my cock through her warmth, coating myself and teasing her clit with the tip, is all sex. When her eyes meet mine, a string hooked to my ribcage pulls taut and draws me closer. Not in a physical way. It's this invisible tether that has always forced me to gravitate to her.

A sense of peace settles inside my chest when I notch my head at her entrance. It grows and spreads through me as I press in, drop my mouth to hers, and swallow her cries. Slowly, I stretch her, forcing her to accommodate me. Each inch that I breach brings us closer until we're one. Until she's clutching my back and digging her heels into my ass.

"That's my good little slut, taking me completely without complaint. Look at you," I mutter as I stare down at our bodies as we rock gently together. "It's like you were made to be fucked by me. Made for my cock and only my cock."

Hooded, glassy eyes lock on me as I slide in and out of her. Slowly, a smile spreads across her face. It's naughty and downright devious. Liquid fire douses my skin as I wait for what she'll say.

"On your back, Ford. That's my cock, and I'm going to ride it."

"Fuck yes, it is," I growl, flipping us so that she's on top. She spreads her legs wider, dropping her hips lower, and screams as she takes me deeper than before. She falls forward and slaps one hand to my stomach to steady herself. And then, like she's riding a goddamn bull, she moves.

Her pussy is a vise, squeezing me in rhythm with her every thrust. Her heat soaks into me, warming my entire body. With a thumb to her clit, I rub circles and relish the way she fucks me with abandon, her hips gyrating, her heels turned up. Her breasts bounce, the pink nipples pebbled and begging to be bitten, and I must obey. I lean up and take one between my teeth, gentle enough not to hurt her but surprising her just the same.

"Yes, Ford, right there," she murmurs.

I don't let up, circling her clit and licking and nipping at her tits while she rides me. I never want this feeling to end. Her hair falls around us, and I'm engulfed in her scent, sugar and sweetness mixed with sex and lust. She's a dichotomy. This sweet girl I want to destroy. The woman beneath the public persona, the hottest fucking tease, the dirtiest little thing, whimpering and begging for me to fuck her until she can't walk.

"You're a dirty little thing, aren't you?" I suck on the flesh of her tit until the spot strawberries, then I find another spot to mark.

"Only for you," she whimpers, grinding her pussy against me.

"That's right, Red. Only for me. Now come all over my cock. Milk me. I want to feel every fucking inch of that pussy, every ridge. I want you to devour me."

As if on command, she does just that, pulsing out her release as she stumbles over the edge into the abyss, taking me with her. It's euphoria. Nothing has ever felt this good.

And I know, without a doubt, nothing ever will.

LAKE
9

LOOK WHAT YOU MADE ME DO

God, I don't want to wake up from this dream. I'm on the precipice of an intense orgasm, though, so while my eyes fight to blink themselves open, my mind tells me to keep them shut so I can enjoy this. With a hum, I glide a hand down my stomach to my apex. Every inch of me comes together, ready to ride this wave for real. But instead of finding the soft warmth of my swollen center, my fingertips brush hair. When I grip the strands, a deep chuckle resonates between my thighs. Teeth nip at my clit, and I buck up in surprise, finally forcing my eyes open. Smiling up at me is the most devastating face, a man songs should be written about, but that I intend to keep to myself.

"Ford," I moan.

I'm rewarded with another nibble. "That's my good girl. Greedy little thing was riding my face while she slept. Now come on my tongue so I can fuck you again before breakfast."

Oh my god. It's the only thing I can think when his tongue delves between my lips and he digs his fingers into my ass to pull me closer while he literally feasts on me. The man eats me like it's his favorite thing to do. And damn, is he good at it. He's quickly making me an addict.

I spiral, clenching my thighs around his head as I come so hard I see stars. My body practically levitates off the bed, spurring him to drape an arm over my stomach to hold me down and force me to take more. "Please, please," I pant. I'm not even sure what I'm begging for.

"Against the window. Hands on the glass," he orders as he stands and goes in search of a condom, I'm guessing.

Still naked from last night, I eye the rumpled blanket draped over the foot of the bed. *Will he let me get away with covering myself?*

Startling me, Ford rasps, "There a problem?"

I shake my head. "I just—" I drop my focus to the sheet covering my body. "*Clothes*—I'm naked, and it's daylight."

Ford's lips tip up into a thoughtful smile. "It is, isn't it? Guess Boston is about to see me destroy the perfect image of their princess."

My thighs clench. This man's words alone are enough to have me teetering on the edge again.

"Tits on the glass, ass spread, begging for my cock. Leave the girl who says please and thank you behind." His words are nothing more than grunts. "Demand your orgasms. Because only I can satisfy that need you have. Right, my little slut? You need my cock..." He grips himself and drags his hand up and down his shaft as he stalks toward me. "Inside you." Without looking away, he spits into his hand and wraps his fingers around his shaft again and works himself over. "Fucking you until you can't walk. *Now, Red.* You have five seconds before I drag you over there, and when I do, there will be consequences."

Heart pounding out of my chest, I scramble out of bed and slam my hands against the cold glass. My nipples are so hard the shock of it almost hurts. Cheek flat so I can keep him in my periphery, I wait for him to touch me. Nerves swarm my belly. Last night was one thing. We'd both been drinking. It was dark. But here in the daylight, there's no hiding what we're doing. I'm about to be fucked by my ex-boyfriend's father while completely sober. And I'm shaking with a need that, as he so aptly pointed out, can only be quelled by him. This moment, these hours, will be branded on my soul and in my brain for the rest of my life. I'll dream about them, get off to them, and mourn them when they're over.

I'm not fool enough to believe this could lead to a happily ever after, but I'll enjoy every freaking moment until it blows up in my face.

Warm hands circle my thigh and guide it, widening my stance. Then for just a moment, Ford presses himself to my back, breathing me in, as if he needs this as much as I do, a reminder that it won't last, this little game we're playing.

Game or not, it might be the truest thing I've ever experienced. I close my eyes when his lips meet my shoulder. "Being able to touch you is unreal, Red. I'm fucking losing my mind right now."

I drop my head back against his chest as he slides his cock between my legs. "Me too," I whisper, my breath unsteady.

He kisses my shoulder again and murmurs in my ear. "I'm going to treat you like my dirty little slut again, but know that it means so much more than that."

His voice is so tender it's almost as if the words are whispered by another person. Because in the same moment, he thrusts in hard, stealing my ability to breathe. Filling me so completely that I don't know where he begins and I end. Fingers dig into my hips as he thrusts relentlessly, the only sounds our joined moans and the slap of his palm against my ass as he fucks me into oblivion.

"Look down, Red. Look at all the people who are always looking up to you."

With my hands flat against the glass, I find the street at least thirty floors below. The people are so small I can barely make out details.

"What would they say if they could see you now? Taking your ex's father's cock. *Revenge*." His dark chuckle makes me shiver while simultaneously sending a wave of heat to my core. "That's what you'd have them believe, but we all know you've wanted this cock since the beginning. That if you could have chosen, you'd have picked me."

His thrusts are punishing, as if he wants me to know just how angry he is that I didn't choose him. It's a game. He never really felt that way. Even if he remembers what I wore the day we met. Why wouldn't he, right? I'm fucking pop royalty, his biggest fucking star. I *made* his career.

"Yes," I play the game too, despite how close to my truth his words hit. Ford is devastatingly good-looking. He intrigued me from that first day too. I just never imagined he'd be interested in me. Too young, too naïve, too proper and perfect. All the qualities he's promised to fuck out of me.

I laugh at the ridiculous turn my thoughts have taken, but the sound only seems to make him angrier, like maybe he thinks I'm laughing at him.

He grasps my throat with one hand and pulls me closer, squeezing slightly. "If you can laugh, I'm not doing my job."

Moaning, I focus on the way he holds me in place, the way we must look, both of us naked; me with my dark hair flowing around us, my body bruised and spent from being used all night, my tits pressed up against the window, my pussy spread and taking the beating his cock is giving me; Ford, the older man with so much strength he could easily subdue me. He could literally hold me down and fuck me, and I couldn't stop him. Just the thought makes me gush, leaving me dripping all over him.

With his free hand, he finds my clit, and in a matter of seconds, I scream out my release.

"That's it, Red. Squeeze me baby. Yes, fuck, you are so perfect, taking my cock like this. Milk me, baby. Take it all." He curses and sinks his teeth into my shoulder as he explodes inside me.

I drop my forehead against the window with a little too much force, sucking in lungfuls of air. Ford doesn't let me pull away. Instead, he holds me close, taking my weight. "Come on, gorgeous, let's get you showered," he murmurs.

Showering with him should be awkward, allowing him such intimate access to my body to wash me, but that feeling never comes. Ford turns on the water, and when he's sure it isn't too hot, he sets me beneath it. Then he washes my hair and caresses my body, cleaning every inch of skin. When he ghosts between my legs, a moan escapes me and heat pools low in my belly.

He forces my mouth up to his and kisses me beneath the spray. "You need to rest, Lake. And eat."

"But that feels so good," I whimper. I'm sore, and purple bruises are already starting to appear all over my body. I love every single discoloration. They mar me, leaving beautiful imperfections that remind me of all we've done over the last few hours. Every moment, every word, every kiss. Each bruise is a memory littered along my body, and I'm already dreading when they're gone.

He drugs me with a kiss, licking at the seam of my lips. There's no purpose, no end goal. He consumes me because he can, melding our mouths together in a way that will ruin me for others. When I try to reach for him, he brushes my hand away. "I'm going to finish up in here. Go get ready, and then we'll have breakfast."

Just as I'm stepping out of the bathroom wrapped in a fluffy white robe, a knock sounds at the door. Maybe he already ordered breakfast to be delivered. He did it last week and already knows what I like. However, when I open the door, I find a professionally dressed woman with dark hair standing on the other side.

"Good morning," she says, holding out a large white shopping bag. "I have a delivery for Mr. Hall."

Hoping she doesn't recognize me—not only am I in my robe and with my hair in a towel turban, but I'm dressed this way in Ford's room —I thank her and take the bag before anyone else spots me and close the door quickly. Once the lock clicks into place, I spin and fall back against the solid wood.

Ford appears, towel circling his waist, his chest and the dark trail down his belly still damp. God, he's gorgeous. His body, the ease with which he carries himself, the confident, intelligent way he speaks. And when he looks at me? Blue eyes warm with affection. Fuck, I'm melting.

"Oh, your clothes arrived."

"Huh?" I'm still dumbstruck at the sight of him.

"You can't wear the dress you had on last night," he says, lips turning up in a wicked smile. "Unless you really want to make a statement. Your choice. I'm good either way."

I swallow. "I repeat, huh?"

"For breakfast. Get dressed." He points to the bag I'd forgotten all about and pulls his towel off. Unabashedly, he stands before me, naked, and runs it against his hair. Leaving his thick cock on display, long and only slightly hard. It should be a crime to be this good-looking at any age, but damn, he's almost twice my age and sexier than any man I've ever seen.

"You want to go to breakfast with me?"

I can't wrap my head around the idea. Sure, we had sex. And maybe we even shared a kiss in public—though it was the most private version of public there is. I'm sure Ford's friends had that party on lockdown from the press. No way would the owners of a hockey team want their players caught on camera on New Year's Eve.

Ford stares at me like I'm an idiot.

"You don't want anyone to know about us," I tell him.

"That was the deal, wasn't it? I don't get the benefit of sinking my cock inside you only to let you walk out like you've done something shameful."

"I'm your son's ex."

"Yeah, my son, who is gallivanting around Bali with your tour manager on *my* dime, not bothering to hide a fucking thing." Red-faced, Ford wraps his towel around his waist again. "I've been teaching him right from wrong all his life. He doesn't follow the rules, he faces the punishment. That's how it's always been."

"So that's what I am? His punishment?" I ask, caught somewhere between feeling wicked and confused.

He steps closer and ducks his head to look me in the eye. "And my reward."

The mix of emotions clears quickly, and I can't hold back my smile. "What are you being rewarded for?"

"Pretty sure the five orgasms I've given you in the last twelve hours have earned me a breakfast date."

Pulling my lip between my teeth, I survey the skyline out the floor-to-ceiling windows. Outside, the world is going about its business. "You really want to take me to breakfast?"

Ford presses closer and swipes a thumb across my chin, back and forth, like he just can't keep himself from touching me. "Yeah, Lake, I want to take you to breakfast."

I sigh, considering the implication, but quickly get lost in his heart-breakingly blue eyes. They're the color of the ocean now. Midnight blue and dangerous. "You do realize what that entails, right? I'm a media circus at all times."

Once again, I apologize for my success. Apologize for being me.

Ford inches closer, his lips tipping up like he's in on a joke. "My label has been in charge of that circus for two years, Red. I'm well aware of what breakfast entails."

"Everyone will know you fucked your son's ex." Our lips are practically touching now, but I keep pushing him away. With my words. With my reality. He's obviously thinking with his dick right now.

Ford arches an unimpressed brow. "And?"

"It's exhausting. This will be all over the internet and plastered on the cover of every magazine in the grocery store checkout. It's one more thing they can print about me, one more way they'll dig into my life."

He rubs his nose against mine. The small gesture makes my heart skip and warmth skitter through every inch of my body. "They'll talk anyway. They'll make up stories. How about you live the life you want? *Fuck,* at least now you're doing things worth talking about."

I bite my lip and shake my head, but I don't pull back. "What about your reputation? It's your label," I whisper.

"And he's my son. If I don't give a fuck, then why should you?" And then his lips are on mine and he's pulling me as close as he can get me. Our tongues tangle and our breaths mingle. My mind whirls with all the potential stories, all the comments and articles that'll paint me in a negative light. But he's right. The media does that already. Now, at least, they'll be true, and I'll have a fucking good time while they talk.

LAKE 10

CALL IT WHAT YOU WANT

Normally, walking out of a hotel feels like a secret mission. Men talking into headsets finding the safest route. Heads bowed, smiles hidden and absolutely no talking or stopping to sign an autograph.

Ford is a different animal. The man stalks out, chin high, proud as a peacock, smiling at me like what we're doing doesn't have the potential to tank his label or piss off his son. Like even if it did, he doesn't give a fuck.

And I'm beginning to believe he truly doesn't. He wasn't giving me lip service to appease me. When he speaks, he doesn't just string letters of the alphabet together like so many people do. He puts thought into what he says, makes calculated decisions, and takes risks.

I haven't taken a risk since I launched my career. Since the moment I had the audacity to send tapes to every person even remotely related to the music industry, hoping that one of them would actually listen and be blown away by my rendition of "Kiss Me" by Six Pence None the Richer.

In the end, what got me onto Music Row in Nashville was singing in a tiny café on open mic night every week, without fail. And waitressing in said café so that I knew precisely when record execs would be there.

Somehow the girl who left home at sixteen to follow her dreams went soft. Or maybe I'd just frozen. My star rose too quickly. All the critics had strong opinions. Whether good or bad, I couldn't get their words out of my head.

So much so that the words that mattered most, my own, had dried up.

Too concerned with upsetting someone with a lyric or being laughed at when I poured my heart out, I allowed others to guide my decisions. First with my wardrobe, then with my music. It's only now that I'm realizing I no longer make even the smallest decisions without the approval of someone at the label.

Until today when Ford said fuck it. Even now, am I using his approval as my guide?

I shrug away that uncomfortable thought, because that's not how this feels. For once, I'm not stifled by someone else's opinion. He's giving me space to choose.

Ford rests a hand on the small of my back as he ushers me down the sidewalk, and that's when I spot the first camera. Used to forcing a smile, I do just that, but as I go into people-pleaser mode, Ford tenses beside me.

I knew it was going to bother him. It isn't easy being photographed at all times. Being forced to always be on.

People who crave the limelight, who only want to spend time with me for the attention they'll get out of it, love the constant spotlight. But people who are more concerned with living genuine lives, who appreciate me for me? Time and time again, this has been the deal-breaker.

Ford grasps my hip and pulls me closer as the photographer calls out to us. "Lake, what's going on?"

And with that, the vultures appear, circling their prey, one squawks, and suddenly more surface.

Another photographer shouts, "Have you heard from Paul?"

"Wait, isn't that his father?" One mutters loud enough to make the others do a double take.

In moments, we're being followed down the street as question after question is lobbed our way.

"What's going on here?"

At the audacity behind those words, I stop in my tracks and whirl around to face the short, pudgy man who asked.

Ford circles my waist and brings his head close to mine. "What are you doing?"

Without breaking my smile, I reply, "Giving them something to talk about."

His breath tickles my ear, but he doesn't object, so I take that as his consent.

"We're headed to breakfast. I'll probably walk on the wild side this morning. Have a bacon, egg, and cheese sandwich with home fries, since I had a few cocktails last night."

When I wink, the paps eat it up, laughing together.

"With your ex-boyfriend's father?" the guy who aptly pointed it out before asks, his tone full of judgment.

I let my jaw drop in an exaggerated shocked expression, then clap a hand over my mouth and, wide-eyed, turn to Ford. "Oh my God, is that who you are?"

With a shake of his head, Ford chuckles, clearly enjoying my impromptu show. He pulls me closer and growls in my ear. "You're in so much trouble, Red." But his eyes dance in delight.

I tap one finger to my lips. "I *did* think he looked familiar." Then, throwing a thumb in his direction, I tease, "He is elderly, though, so he might have forgotten who I am."

Ford squeezes my ass. "I'll fucking show you elderly." His breath is hot on my neck, and the rumble of his voice sends a pulse of desire through me. Then, affecting a bored expression, he looks at the guys. "Anything else?"

"Are you two dating now?" Both men look from Ford to me and back again, eyes wide and mouths agape.

I never answer questions. Even if I did, I don't have an answer for that one.

Ford grins wickedly. "A gentleman never kisses and tells." He turns to me, cups my cheek, and whispers, "But no one has ever called me a gentleman." Then his lips are locked with mine and his tongue slides inside my mouth. He's making it clear to the entire world that he's a man of his word. He doesn't give a fuck.

AFTER BREAKFAST, we head back to the hotel, where we watch hours of television, order in dinner, and talk late into the night. Naked, of course. With lots of kissing and touching and orgasms for us both. My next show isn't for two weeks, and I have no concrete plans. Paul and I were supposed to go home to LA to recharge, but the last thing I want to do is surround myself with reminders of him. So when Ford asks me to spend another night, I let the girl who used to take risks answer.

Why not hide away and get lost in one another for a little longer?

Only, he has other plans. The following day, he gets us both packed up and ushers me to the car. We're halfway there before I realize he's taking me to his home. By the time we pull into the driveway, the weight pressing against my chest makes it hard to breathe. The last time I walked into this house, I was celebrating Christmas with Ford and his son. The man that, until a few days ago, was my boyfriend. The man I've yet to hear from since I caught him with his lips wrapped around my tour manager's dick.

I'm afraid to ask Ford if he's heard from him. His other children have called, though he hasn't hinted at how they reacted to the news of their father kissing their brother's ex-girlfriend. It's all sort of a mess.

Mel was obviously thrilled. My mother and father, not so much. I didn't put nearly enough thought into the fact that everyone in my life would know what we'd done the moment we walked out of the hotel together, but that is precisely what happened, and it's too late to change it now. I'm just trying to ignore it for the time being. Honestly, the Ford-induced orgasms may have some sort of mind-numbing effect, because I've clearly lost any sense of self-preservation and smarts.

The moments with him outside of the bedroom are equally incredible and confusing, because despite our age difference, he gets me. We laugh over the same jokes, enjoy the same shows, and he has this innate ability to sense what I need before I even realize I need it.

Like right now. We're side by side at the table. He's got his laptop out, reviewing a contract. I've got a notepad in front of me, and I'm working out lyrics that have just popped into my head. When I get pulled in like this, I typically make myself a cup of hot tea. But before I even have a chance to get up and go in search of a mug, he's sliding one in front of me.

He smiles at my look of surprise. "You didn't even hear me making it."

"Thank you." I take a sip and allow the warmth to ease my throat. My vocal cords are going to need a rest before the tour picks up again. All these orgasms wreak as much havoc on them as a full set list does.

Buttons rubs against me, and when I reach down and scratch her head, she purrs in delight.

"How's the song coming along?" He juts his chin toward my paper.

For the first time in maybe ever, I don't feel the compulsion to hide the words. The label has more influence over my music than I'd like already, so I normally keep this part of my process private. Just for me. I don't want input on the market or what sounds are popular to influence my songwriting.

Ford Hall owns the label, yes, but this Ford, the man who is wearing sweats and a white T-shirt and his black-framed glasses, with his hair mussed from our midday romp, doesn't make me uneasy.

I'm not sure what we are to one another, no idea what I'd even call it if I was asked, but he makes me comfortable. His eyes create a melody in my head, leaving my body humming along with my lips.

An ache eases in my chest as the tune swirls around us and fills the room. A tune we've been creating together. One he's nurtured through his sweet, simple nature.

If Ford is surprised that I'm serenading him with a song about two people engaging in an affair that, to the outside world, is considered taboo, all while feeling so made for one another, so at ease, he doesn't let it show. The thoughtful smile he wears isn't one of a man who knows this could be his label's next hit. It's the knowing smile of a man who understands the complexity behind my simple lyrics. As if the thoughts that are running through my head—that we fit in a way that makes no sense and yet all the sense in the world—are not one-sided.

As I finish, he drops his head and gives it a shake, as if he's coming out of a dream. Like maybe he believes this is all a dream. It very well could be. If dreams leave you sore in the space between your thighs and make your limbs ache for the person right beside you.

"You give words to the unspoken, Red. Don't ever stop wearing your heart on your sleeve."

There's something so telling about that statement. He didn't say the song was perfect—a word I've come to hate—he didn't focus on what the critics will have to say about the song or how it will be received by fans. Ford did what he always does: he saw into my deepest insecurities. He reached in and grabbed Lake, the woman hiding behind them, waiting to be seen, and he spoke to *her*.

He spoke to me like my music does daily.

I'm so screwed.

The air around us is quiet now that I've stopped singing, but his words play on repeat in my mind and hit me like a shot to the heart. Then he goes and smiles, and that beautiful ache suddenly morphs to a lightness I've never experienced.

"C'mere, Red." He pats his knee.

I try to hold back my smile. "You want me to sit on your lap?"

"What I *want* is to take you over to the couch and have my way with you, but considering I'm an old man and we've had sex four times today, I'll settle for cuddling you instead."

With a laugh, I curl up on his lap and nuzzle into the space below his chin. "You're not that old."

His carefree laugh pulls me in further, like quicksand. I'll never be able to dig myself out. And maybe I don't want to.

Perhaps jealous of the cuddles I'm getting from her dad, Buttons jumps up onto my lap and rubs her head against my chest. Ford offers her a little attention, rubbing at her fur.

"You all done with work for the day?" I ask, closing my eyes.

He presses a kiss to my forehead. "Just have to send one more e-mail. Why don't you go put a bathing suit on? We can relax in the hot tub once I'm done."

Nibbling on my lip, I pull back. "Don't have one."

His eyes track the way I lick across my lips. "Remember the last time we were in the hot tub, Red?"

God, that nickname sends a shock of need through me every time. Need almost as strong as the kind that courses through me at the memory he's conjuring. I nod. "Yeah, Paul ditched me on my birthday, and you scared the shit out of me. I thought I had the house to myself."

"You were naked."

Memories of that night flood me, along with a wave of liquid heat. I'm not sure why I thought skinny-dipping in Ford's hot tub was a good idea. Though, to be fair, he was supposed to be out of town, and Paul and I were supposed to have a romantic night at home to celebrate my birthday. I'd been invited to a club—hell, there were parties everywhere in my honor—but I hate stuff like that. A quiet night at home where I could be myself was all I wanted. Paul insisted one of us should make an appearance, so he took off. I stayed home with a bottle of bubbly and my guitar. I didn't have a suit, but the hot tub looked so inviting. Ford's house was secluded, with high privacy fences, so I assumed I'd be safe to relax.

I climbed in wearing white undies and a bra, but the way they clung to my skin when they were wet was gross, so I dumped them by the steps and sank below the surface, leaving nothing between me and the bubbles.

And then he walked outside…

"Bought you a suit in case it ever happened again." His rough voice pulls me out of the past.

I'd much rather be in the present anyway. Because the way he affects me is no longer a problem. Or at least not as much of a problem as it was when I was naked in Ford's hot tub while still in a relationship with his son and I saw him without a shirt on for the first time. God, if I hadn't been so freaked out that he would be angry about me in my birthday suit, I probably would have enjoyed the view.

But there's nothing stopping me now.

"You want me to wear a bathing suit?" I tease.

Ford pulls his glasses off and sets them on the table purposefully. Then he cups my face, running his fingers against my cheek. "Play along, Red. Bathing suit is on the bed upstairs. Put it on. I'll leave champagne outside. Go out there. Relax for a bit. Maybe relive that night…though with a different outcome."

My mind whirs to life at what he's suggesting, and heat pools between my legs. I'm in such a hurry to obey I practically tumble out of his lap, and Buttons jumps at the last minute so she doesn't fall to the ground.

Ford laughs and grasps my hips, steadying me in front of him. "Dirty girl is already wet just thinking about fucking her boyfriend's father, isn't she?"

Oh my God.

Before my mind goes into overdrive and stops me from playing a game I am far too eager to engage in, I jump in with both feet. "And you're the man who can't stop thinking about fucking your son's girl-friend." I run one fingertip from his jawline, down his neck, to the collar of his T-shirt. "Knowing nothing will feel better than my tight cunt."

With that, I spin on my heel and scamper up the stairs.

"Fuck." His growl echoes in the silent house.

Damn right. That's exactly what I intend to do.

Two scraps of white fabric barely big enough to be considered a bikini await me. Hands shaking, I shuck my clothes and shimmy into it, then blow out a long breath and pull my shoulders back. I need a steady hand to apply my red lipstick. On the duvet beside the indecent bikini is a single hair tie. I consider not using it, only because I love the way Ford takes care of me and the idea of him finding it, sliding it onto his wrist, and then putting it in my hair makes my stomach flip and my skin flush hotter. But in the end, we're playing a game—one where I look like I did that night—so my hair goes up.

Guitar in hand, I pad down the stairs to a quiet house. Ford is seemingly MIA, and I can't help but smile to myself. He's really set this up to mimic that night.

When I step outside, the cold hits me immediately. Strings of twinkling lights illuminate the backyard, and two lines of solar lights lead to the already bubbling hot tub. With a deep breath, I brace myself for the cold and grasp the neck of my guitar tight, then take off down the short path.

"Shit, shit, shit!" The chill that immediately envelops me is impossible to ignore. Halfway there, my toes are going numb. Should have put my shoes back on or snooped around for a pair of slippers.

Gently, I set my guitar on the edge beside a small stack of towels and dip a toe into the water. I pull back quickly and let out an "Ah!" It's a lot hotter than I remembered. Probably because my toes are frozen now.

Letting out a deep breath, I ease into the water. It only takes a moment to adjust to the heat, and when I do, I drop my head back against the headrest in one corner and allow my muscles to relax. It's been such a long few weeks. If not for the games I'm playing with Ford, I'd probably already be in LA, hiding from the gossip surrounding Paul's affair.

It's strange how little I've thought of him—outside of his relation to Ford and the repercussions there. Normally a breakup would send me into a tailspin. I'd write sad songs for weeks and wallow in my misery. But that hasn't happened. I'm just…content. Or distracted maybe. Because the man I'm sleeping with is one hell of a distraction.

I stare at my guitar, wondering if I have another song in me. The days after a breakup are sometimes my most inspired, even if the songs revolve around heartbreak and pain. Oddly, the only things that are going through my head are words about comfort and a warmth I didn't know existed inside me. Lovely lyrics that would make listeners think I'm falling in love rather than exacting a little revenge.

I spot the champagne and smile to myself. On my birthday, I drank straight from the bottle.

Apparently he remembered too, because the glasses are missing.

Feeling wicked, I kneel on the bench seat on the other side of the tub and snag the bottle. It takes a few seconds to work the metal trap and wrapper off, but when I do, I give in to the little devil on my shoulder and give the bottle a good shake before I press on the cork with my thumb. It goes flying, and a fountain of champagne erupts from the bottle. The laugh that escapes me as it coats my upper body is loud and long.

"Lake?"

Startled, I spin, the smile still on my face, bottle in hand and over-flowing into the hot tub.

His expression is nothing like what I expected. The warm, effusive man is gone. Now he's looking at me the way he used to. He's the detached CEO, friendly but not smoldering.

My stomach sinks, yet my heart pounds out a rhythm in my chest, the two reactions in complete juxtaposition to one another, as I take him in. The cold champagne running down my arm reminds me of the mess I'm making. Shit. I slide the mouth of the bottle between my lips in an attempt to stop the liquid from overflowing into his hot tub.

"Shit, sorry," I say, pulling the bottle away and swiping at the excess liquid on my lips. The champagne burns a line of bubbles down my throat and goes straight to my head. Or maybe the dizziness that hits me is from the lust that's soaking through my body at the way Ford is looking at me.

Why is the detached expression doing it for me? Furrowed brow, slight frown, not quite cold eyes, but not warm either? Yep. Every bit of it. It's exactly how he looked at me the night he found me just like this so many months ago...

He locks his jaw and lets his gaze track down my body. I dip my chin and follow the path he takes. There's a trickle of champagne still slowly making its way between my breasts and red smudges on one hand. Shit. My lipstick. It's probably smudged around my mouth too.

But when I go to wipe at it, Ford's sharp command stops me. "Leave it."

"Sorry." I drop my hand and peer up at him. "I thought I was alone."

His attention is still locked firmly on me. "Where's my son?"

Holy shit, we're really doing this.

Lowering my lashes, I throw back another gulp of champagne, then hold it out to him.

He's still looming over the hot tub, sweats sitting low on his hips, torso bare, muscles flexing as he folds his arms across his chest.

"He went out."

With a shake of his head, he tuts. "He left you on your birthday?"

Since he hasn't taken the offered champagne, I tip it back once more, then set the bottle behind me and dip under the water before replying. "It's okay. I didn't want to go out. Just wanted to relax."

Ford sighs heavily. "I'll let you be, then." Without another word, he stuffs his hands into the pockets of his sweatpants and turns back toward the house.

The water sloshes as I sit up quickly. "Wait!"

His steps falter, and for a moment, he stands still with his back to me. When he looks at me over his shoulder, he's got one brow arched. "Need something?"

More than anything, I want to blurt out *yes, your cock*, but we're playing a game, and we both know I'll get that soon enough. "Um, it's your hot tub. I don't want to intrude." Water sluices down my body as I stand. "I can go inside so you can have it all to yourself."

Ford hisses and roughs a hand down his face. "Sit down."

"I'm sorry?"

"Your bathing suit," he grits out. "It's…" He presses one hand to his forehead and averts his eyes while he waves the other hand up and down, gesturing to my body. "I can see everything."

All the air leaves my lungs as I glance down at myself. Sure enough, the bathing suit is, in fact, completely see-through. That dirty man. I almost laugh, but I pull myself together instead and continue with my role. Biting my lip, I reply, "I'm so sorry, Mr. Hall. I didn't realize anyone would be home."

"I find that hard to believe." His voice is harder now, and he's stalking toward me. The air is so cold I should be shivering, but the heat from the water and the way his gaze sears my skin keep me standing. His attention dips to my nipples and holds as he steps up to the edge of the tub. "I think you knew precisely what you were doing."

The words cut through the air. Aren't they the truth? Since the moment I asked Ford to kiss me on the dance floor, I've known. Or at least I thought I did.

Now I'm starting to wonder if my pretense was just that. Have I always wanted this with him? Did I ignore the desire because of our professional relationship and our age difference? It isn't hard to reimagine the last time we met like this. Only when I do, I let myself see him for who he really is, and I allow my deepest, most hidden longings to bubble to the surface. Maybe I *have* always lusted after my boyfriend's father.

Either way, I can't imagine going back to that moment and not finding him irresistible. I must have seen it.

"I—" I glance down and watch as he swipes a thumb against my pebbled nipple. The white fabric clings to my wet skin, making the pink beneath it obvious.

"Be honest, Lake, you sent Paul out tonight in hopes that I'd find you out here. Alone." He swallows thickly and looks me up and down. "Like this."

His words scrape at me. He might as well have licked between my thighs for how wet I am.

"N-no. That's not—" I shake my head and take a step back. The water tickles my skin as it bubbles around my legs. "I'll just go inside."

"Please sit. You shouldn't be alone on your birthday."

With a sigh, I take another step back, intent on settling beneath the surface. I'll keep my body hidden like I would have back then. Like I did. Because that night, I was naked beneath the bubbles. Though back then, I thought Ford hadn't noticed.

"Wait," he says, grasping my arm. When he pulls me close, his eyes are slits.

I blink up at him. "Is there something wrong?"

"You're still covered in champagne." He says it like he's angry about it. "It's going to get in the hot tub if you sit back down."

"And?"

"And it'll fuck with the chemicals."

I almost giggle, because it absolutely will not fuck with the chemicals and I've already dipped below the surface once. Instead, I give him a look of feigned shock. "Oh, should I get out and clean off first?"

He shakes his head and presses up against the side of the tub. "No —just let me…" Dipping his head, he closes his mouth around the swell of my breast and sucks. Then he licks at my chest. The feel of his tongue, warm and soft, is such a contrast to the frigid air. His steely gaze remains fixed on me as he cleans me with his tongue.

When a moan slips out, he peeks up and smirks. "You're not supposed to enjoy that."

"I'm not supposed to enjoy the feeling of your hot tongue on my body?"

"You're not supposed to enjoy having your boyfriend's father's hot tongue on your body," he reminds me.

Lust races through my veins, making my knees wobble. It's wicked the way I feel right now.

"You're a dirty little thing, aren't you?" he says. His eyes are hard, but the tiny smirk playing on his lips gives away precisely how he feels.

"No," I lie. "I'm sorry."

"You can sit now." He releases me and pulls back.

Disappointment ricochets through me when cool air rushes between us, but I obey, settling into the molded seat behind me while I watch him slip off his sweats. I salivate as I wait to see what he's got on under them. The night he caught me in the hot tub, he was wearing board shorts. I assumed he didn't know I was naked, otherwise he wouldn't have climbed in across from me. Then, I sat low in hopes he wouldn't notice while I tried my best to not stare at his chiseled chest.

Now, I wish I was naked. I wish we both were.

When Ford slides his thumbs beneath his waistband and drags his sweats down his thighs, breath hisses from my lips. He's completely fucking naked and hard as a rock.

"Working on any songs lately?"

The subject change throws me. I try not to gawk at him, but my body is on fire.

Making a tsking noise, he shakes his head and grabs himself. "Now look what you've done." He runs his hand up his shaft and circles the head with his thumb. His gaze snaps to mine. "What would your boyfriend think if he came home and saw how hard you've made me? You're going to have to take care of this before he gets here."

My pussy clenches so violently I squeeze my thighs together to soothe the ache. "Take care of it? Wouldn't it look worse if he caught me touching you?"

He lets out a low grunt. "He won't see anything because my cock will be shoved down your throat." The water splashes as he steps into the tub and stalks across the bench until he's looming over me, his cock in his hand. "Open."

I scramble to my knees for a better angle, my pussy spasming in anticipation. His words alone will be the death of me.

"Those goddamn red lips. I can't tell you how many times I've pictured them circling my cock while you suck me down."

I press a kiss to the head, staining his flesh with my lipstick. Then I swirl my tongue around it, teasing him a bit.

He grunts. "Open that fucking mouth, Red."

Peering up at him, I obey, smiling around him as he slides inside. He doesn't go easy on me. He grasps the back of my head to hold me in place and pushes all the way to the back of my throat.

"Fuck...this mouth is famous for all the wrong things."

His face is cast in shadow as he slides his hand from the back of my head down and along my neck until he's cupping my chin and rubbing a thumb against my cheek softly. "You feel like heaven."

It's a momentary break in the game we've been playing. But it doesn't make the scene any less hot. Arguably the most powerful man in the music industry is looking at me like what we're doing is so much more than a dirty fantasy. Like my mouth and what it's doing are not what he's referring to. Like maybe, just maybe, *we're* more than a dirty fantasy.

But thoughts like that have never led me anywhere good. Believing any man who shows an interest in me wants long-term commitment is stupid. Thinking this could be more than a fling would be stupid. So I grip his base and start moving. Sucking and licking and lapping at him while he curses about how fucking amazing I am, about how good my mouth feels and how he's about to come down my throat.

The way he calls me his dirty little slut sends a shiver of excitement down my spine, and when he finishes with a curse and pulls me down into the hot tub to kiss me, I ignore the pangs of need I'm inundated with. Not lust-filled need, but the need to be held. To escape in his kisses. They're long and brutal and taste like sin.

Like him.

When it becomes too much, when the drug threatens to take me under, I push off and settle back into my role. "Better stay over there. Otherwise your son might come home to find you fucking his girlfriend."

Ford lifts his chin and peruses me with an aloof expression, but in one quick movement, he lifts me onto the ledge of the hot tub. "Good girl, so long as he doesn't kiss you, he'll never know how hard your sexy little body makes me."

I'm so fucking turned on I don't feel the cold air kissing my skin. His gaze on the space between my thighs is just as wicked as his words.

Will he eat me right here? My heart stumbles at the thought. I can't help but peer over at the window to the room I've always occupied in the past. With Paul. Obviously, we're alone, but Ford chuckles as if he knows precisely what I'm thinking.

"We're not doing anything wrong, Lake," he soothes. "I'm sitting in the hot tub, and you're going to play a song for me."

I blink at him, surprised. "You want me to play for you?"

"Yes. The one from earlier." This time there's a hint of warmth in his tone.

I reach for my guitar, but before I can settle it on my thighs, Ford grabs a towel and pats my skin dry. Even within this game, he's doing things for me, watching out for me, taking care of me.

"Lose the top," he instructs, the harsh tone at odds with the tender gesture.

"Huh?" The conflicting sentiments have me reeling.

"Take off that fucking tease of a top, Lake. Don't get your guitar wet."

I set the guitar behind me again, and with my eyes on him, I bring a hand behind my back and untie the strings. The top loosens around my breasts, but the wet fabric clings to my skin. Ford grunts, signaling me to undo the one around my neck. When I do, he snatches the suit from my body and fists it tight.

"You have the most amazing tits." A rough breath escapes him.

Oh god. My breasts feel heavy under his stare, my pink nipples hard.

"Open your legs."

I don't hesitate to comply.

"Are you wet from sucking me off?" He says it almost introspectively, like he's truly considering the possibility.

"Maybe." I'm breathless and aching for him to find out.

"Slide the fabric over, Red." He roughs a hand down his face. "Let me see."

He's mere inches from my center as I use one finger to slide the fabric to the side and expose myself to him.

"Fuck," he mutters. He shakes his head and peers up at me. "You're dripping for me. We can't leave the evidence."

Without warning, he dives in and slides his tongue along my slit. The warmth of his mouth leaves me bucking back and moaning. When he sucks on my clit, I cry out.

"*Shh*, Red. I'm just cleaning up this mess." And then he goes to work, licking and sucking and making me even wetter.

With another cry of ecstasy, I grasp the hair at the back of his head and ride his face.

Ford pushes back, and with steady hands, he unties my bathing suit. "You aren't even trying to hide anymore," he grits out. "You're sitting here naked and grinding that greedy pussy all over my face."

"Please," I beg. "I need you to fuck me."

Shaking his head, he stands and grabs a towel. He dries my body first and wraps me in a second dry towel, then takes care of himself. And with a flourish, he scoops me into his arms and strides into the house. "I need you in my bed."

At the top of the stairs, I can't help but glance at the closed door that leads to Paul's room. "We've got to be quiet," I whisper. "Wouldn't want to get caught."

Ford growls as he pushes into his bedroom. "No." He tosses me onto the bed. "Let him hear you scream. Maybe then he'll finally know what it sounds like when you come."

FORD
11

I DID SOMETHING BAD

Until last week, I'd prided myself on my ability to control almost everything in my life. There wasn't much that tempted me—not a music deal that I'd spend too much on because of ridiculous notions of a passion project, not by the flashiest of cars, and never by a woman. But the temptress in front of me? She's stolen all my control. What was once a string so taut it threatened to snap every time she opened those pretty red lips is now two shredded pieces, flapping in the wind.

Lake fucking owns me, and she isn't for sale.

Leaving her naked and writhing on my bed, I stalk to my drawer. She was so close to coming I could taste it. I left her balancing on the precipice when I stopped us outside.

Fuck, I've lost my goddamn mind, taking her out in the open like that. My property is secluded and the trees and fencing keep it even more hidden, but still, it was reckless.

I'll never get into my hot tub again without picturing her sucking my cock.

Or the dirty way I took her as if she wasn't mine for the taking.

She definitely is. The girl is as in this as I am. But the game we've been playing tonight? The one where she belongs to him, but I steal a taste anyway? Yeah, that makes me a dirty fucking scoundrel.

She makes me a dirty scoundrel.

It should feel wrong, pretending she's still my son's girlfriend. But he's an ass and he doesn't care, so why should I? We're not hurting anyone. Just playing out a little kink that apparently turns us both on.

Here, now, with her brown hair fanned out on my pillow and her lips swollen from sucking me off, with her hard pink nipples on display and her legs spread, she's a goddamn vision.

As I roll the condom on, she whimpers and runs her fingers over her swollen sex. "Need you."

"Say it louder, Lake. Tell me how much you need my cock. How it's *my cock* you get off on. My cock that makes you come."

Tongue gliding across her lips, she shudders. "Yes, Ford," she purrs. "Your cock is the only one to ever make me feel this way."

Fuck, that word, *cock*, from her beautiful mouth? It knocks me back. The world sees her as a sweet, demure star, but I know better. And fuck if it doesn't make me stand taller, knowing I'm the only one who gets to see her this way.

I kneel on the bed and shuffle closer. "Hold yourself open for me."

She obeys, spreading herself. Her back bows off the bed when I slide my cock between her lips, coating it in her desire.

"Fuck, Ford, why does this feel so good?" Her voice is pained, desperate.

She's a damn siren, pulling me closer. Unable to resist, I dip my head and devour her mouth. Forgetting the games and the commands, I thrust inside her and swallow her responding moan along with anything else she's willing to give me.

We fuck like we can't get enough of one another. Like we'll be torn apart if we don't hold tight. Her nails dig into my ass as she thrusts her hips to match my pace.

"You feel so good, Lake. I'm never going to get enough of this tight little cunt. Of the way you squeeze me. Of your sounds."

She bites my lip as she spasms around me, then throws herself back and screams through her orgasm. Every pulse around me sends me closer to the edge. I want to hold out. I don't want this to end. But I can't fight the wave crashing over me. When my balls draw up tight, I know I've lost the battle. So I squeeze my glutes and set a punishing pace to the finish line. But she's coming with me. With my thumb, I find her clit and circle it. "Come for me again, Red. Give me one more."

"I—can't," she cries beneath me. Only her pussy is telling me another story. As if on command, it pulses around me again.

"Yes, you can. With anyone else, maybe you couldn't, but this greedy pussy wants to come for me one more time. Don't hold back now, my dirty little slut. Give it to me. It's mine. *You're mine.*"

Lake grasps the sheets on either side of her and clenches down on me. I have to physically fight to keep my eyes open to watch her hurtle over the edge, then I'm spilling inside her. The orgasm is more intense than any I've ever experienced. It reaches every inch of my body, but more than that, it hits my heart, leaving it beating erratically just for her.

That's what she's made me. Erratic. Crazy. And so fucking gone for her.

I collapse beside her and suck in a lungful of air, then another, before I have the wherewithal to toss the condom into the bin beside my bed and pull her onto my chest. She's breathing just as heavily as I am, and her heart pounds out its own rhythm against mine. For a long moment, my heartbeat is so loud in my own ears I can't think straight.

The quiet lasts so long I get worried that maybe I pushed her too far. "Lake," I murmur, looking down at her.

She tilts her head back so those stunning blue eyes are locked on me. "Yeah?"

"You okay?"

She gives me a sleepy smile. "Perfect. Just a little tired."

"Bathroom, then sleep," I say, pulling her up and carrying her to the en suite.

Lake giggles in my arms, her body warm and soft against my chest. "You don't have to carry me everywhere."

When I set her on the rug in front of the vanity, I nod to the toilet and lift one brow.

Crossing her arms over her chest, she frowns. "I'm not going to the bathroom with you in here."

A chuckle escapes me. We've explored one another's bodies and minds and fantasies. Yet that's a step too far for her. "Let me brush my teeth, then I'll leave you to yourself."

When I'm finished, I rifle through a drawer and find a brand-new toothbrush for her, then I give her privacy. I take advantage of the moment and head downstairs in search of my phone. Unfortunately, I have an early morning, so I need to set my alarm and check my e-mails to make sure everything is set for my meetings.

I take a minute to check my texts too. Daniel wants to know if we're still on for the game later this week. There's nothing new from Millie, and she still hasn't responded to my last message. She wasn't thrilled about the stories involving Lake and me floating all over the internet. Hopefully Daniel can talk to her.

As for my other son, I have a single unread message from him that reads *Seriously?*

Not sure how Lake would feel about that.

His thoughts on it weren't enough to warrant a phone call.

Idiot.

When I step into my room, Lake is sitting cross-legged on my bed. She doesn't look up from her phone. Like she's pretending to be really into whatever she's looking at.

"Everything okay?" she mumbles, her head still bowed and her shoulders slumped.

I plug my phone into the charger next to the bed, check the alarm once more, and slide between the sheets, wrapping an arm around her midsection and pulling her closer as I do. "All good. Just checking messages from my kids and setting my alarm for tomorrow. I have an early morning."

Lake tenses beside me. "Right," she says, still sitting up and averting her gaze. "I'll arrange for a car to take me back to Boston."

"Why?"

"You have to work," she says slowly, like that makes all the sense in the world. "I'll pick up my stuff, then I'll probably head to New York for the rest of the week."

My heart sinks. I knew it was coming. I can't keep her forever. But I'm not ready to let her go.

"Or you could stay," I say softly, studying her, waiting to dissect her reaction.

She sits a little straighter and finally looks at me. "Stay?"

"You seem relaxed here. Why not stay and take a break? No one will bother you. The paps can't get near my place," I reason, really trying to sell the idea.

"Ford, my parents' house is just as secure."

With a nod, I drop my gaze. Why would she want to stay here? She's probably itching to meet up with Melina...to get back to her life. I'm fucking this up. Security has nothing to do with why I want her to stay.

Speak now. If I don't, I'll be smacking myself later.

"Then stay for me."

"Stay?" she questions again, like she's buying time while she processes the implications and whether she wants to agree.

Though I shouldn't force her to make the decision now, I don't look away. I want her to want me. I want her to stay because she wants to be with me too.

I push her onto her back and hover over her, caging her beneath me. Then I lower my lips to hers and plead my case. "Stay until you have to go back on tour. Stay with me."

She doesn't give me words, but I don't need them when her mouth opens and she kisses me. That's the only answer I need. The one I crave. Her honesty. The real Lake admitting that the connection between us is exactly what I think it is.

There's no urgency to her kiss, because we have time. And that's exactly what I'm desperate for. More time with her. More kisses. More nights between her thighs. *More her.*

LAKE 12

SO IT GOES...

Early every morning, a car arrives and whisks Ford away. While he's at work, I spend my days exploring Bristol. His house is on the water, and along the shore is a bike path that leads directly to a beautiful park and downtown area. Even in the winter, the town keeps the path clear of ice and snow, and the fresh air does me good.

I spend most of my time working on music, but by day three, I'm getting cabin fever, and walking by the water isn't going to cut it, so I head into town.

With the red beanie that Paul gave Ford pulled over my hair and my red scarf wrapped around my neck, I'm almost unrecognizable. Especially when I skip my signature red lipstick and throw on a pair of sunglasses.

The main street is adorable. Every building is decorated for Christmas, even though it's the first week of January. The vibe is very Dickens. Quaint and scenic and crisp. When I stroll past a sign advertising homemade donuts in the window of a bakery, I can't resist. Inside the shop—*Jules*, according to the sign—I'm greeted by a pretty redhead who tells me she's got a fresh batch coming out in a few minutes. She suggests a warm drink while I wait, and I pick a chai tea. Once she slides the paper cup across the counter, I sit at a table in the corner and people watch.

Two guys wearing Bristol Fire Department jackets enter a few moments later, their banter livening up the quiet shop.

"Where's Jules?" the shorter guy asks the other.

The other guy, who looks suspiciously like Shawn Chase, the Dodgers' pitcher who got injured a few years ago and disappeared from the spotlight, rounds the counter and whistles. "Red, you here?"

The nickname has me perking up. I love that Ford calls me that. That the sentiment belongs to just us.

Only it looks as though it belongs to this couple as well.

Strangely, it makes my heart flutter. It's like Ford and I are a normal couple. I haven't been normal for close to ten years. That feeling is magnified when neither man even gives me a second glance.

The taller guy pushes through a swinging door and steps out carrying the redhead over his shoulder in, adorably, a fireman's carry.

She laughs and screeches the whole way. "Shawn, put me down!"

Oh my God. That *is* Shawn Chase. If anyone understands the need for anonymity, it's me, so I say nothing when his girlfriend delivers a white box full of fresh donuts to my table. "Sorry about that. The boys get crazy sometimes."

With a smile, I stand and slip the box into the bag she offers me. "It's sweet. Thank you again." I leave feeling lighter.

The aroma of the warm donuts is so damn tempting, and I'm just considering taking one out for a sample bite when I spot a flower shop with gorgeous arrangements in the window. The shop is outfitted in teal, pink, and purple pastels and calls to me just as fervently as the bakery did. I step inside, set on picking up a bouquet to put on the table for dinner. Maybe I'll pop into the grocery store I noticed down the block next so I can try my hand at cooking tonight. Each night, when Ford appears, he's equipped with takeout, but the idea of surprising him with a home-cooked meal to thank him for all he's done for me makes me giddy.

I've never been so seen or supported. Not to mention the sex. And the orgasms.

Especially the orgasms. I never knew sex could be so explosive. I've been writing about it for years, but now I finally understand what my friends have been saying all along.

Sex with Ford is anything but boring.

"Be right with you." The muffled words come from somewhere on one side of the shop.

Just inside the door, I pause and take a deep breath, filling my lungs with the sugary sweet scent. The entire store is bright. Even the floor is a light pink. Greenery hangs from baskets high up in corners, and ivy snakes the walls.

A little overheated, I slide my hat off my head as I wander. It only takes a minute to spot the perfect bouquet. It's all golds and reds that fit the vibe Ford and I have quickly adopted. With my heart floating in my chest, I grab it and bring it up to the register.

"Find everything you need?" a woman asks as she makes her way toward me from the other side of the shop. When she strolls behind the glass case and catches sight of me, her eyes double in size. And so do mine.

"Amelia Pearson!" I shout in surprise.

"Lake! What the heck are you doing here?" Without hesitation, she comes around the counter and engulfs me in a hug. Amelia is not a hugger, so I appreciate the warm welcome.

I met Amelia in Nashville eons ago, when she and her boyfriend and I were playing in bars, hoping to be seen. Though those years weren't always easy, I look back on them now with nothing but fondness. I'm a few years younger than they are, and I got picked up not long after I met them. But Amelia and Nate, who is now her husband, recently released an album with three number-one hits on it. Their star shot right to the top, though they've yet to tour or make many public appearances. And here she is, in this tiny coastal town. To say I'm surprised to see her would be an understatement.

"What are *you* doing here is the better question." I step back and squeeze her arm.

With a soft smile, she wanders back to the register and waves a hand around the store. "This is my flower shop."

"What?"

"You know me. I don't love the limelight. I agreed to do the whole music thing with Nate so long as we lived in this town and he didn't force me to give this up." She presses her hand against the counter, and instantly, her body relaxes. As if the simple touch has the power to ground her. "Now tell me, what are you doing here?"

"I'm sure you've seen the news…"

Amelia frowns and tilts her head. "I don't really follow all of that."

"Oh." I take in a deep breath and go for it. "Paul cheated on me with my tour manager, so I hooked up with his father to get back at him."

Amelia sucks in a breath and immediately falls into a coughing fit. Yes, it sounds ridiculous when I put it like that. All I can do is laugh as I pat her on the back.

"Oh my God. I so did not expect that," she says, flattening her palm to her chest. With her other hand, she wipes at her eyes, and when she straightens, she beams at me. "But girl, that is the best thing I've heard in a while. My friend Hailey would worship you for that."

"She sounds like a good time," I chirp.

My old friend grins. "She sure is. How long are you in town? You should come over to Thames on Friday. Nate likes to play for the crowd, and then they do open mic night. It's how we test out new music."

The dread that hits me must be evident on my face, because she holds out her hand. "Not for you to perform. But you know, like old times. Hang out, have a drink, listen to good music. Some of the kids who show up are so good. It brings me back," she admits.

When she puts it that way, it does sound nice. I find myself nodding even though I'm not even sure I'll still be here on Friday. Ford and I haven't discussed an expiration date. When will our little fantasy run its course?

Just the thought has my stomach in knots.

"Maybe. That actually doesn't sound awful."

Amelia laughs and picks up a coat from the back counter. "Nate's over at the bar now. Let me put up a closed sign and we can go have lunch. He's going to be thrilled to see you."

I take a step back and wring my hands as all the consequences of showing my face in public like that flash through my mind.

She slides one arm into her coat, then the other, then pats my arm. "Don't worry, the people here are used to seeing celebrities. They don't bat an eye. Except Carmella. She sometimes freaks Shawn and Nate out. She's always asking to squeeze their muscles, but to be fair, she does that to all the guys in town."

"Who's Carmella?"

Amelia smirks. "You'll know her when you see her. She wears muumuus with crazy sayings. I'm pretty sure yesterday's said something like *It's just a joke, not a dick. Don't take it so hard.*"

I let out a loud laugh and allow Amelia to loop her arm through mine and lead me to the bar. Suddenly, this charming town just got a heck of a lot more intriguing.

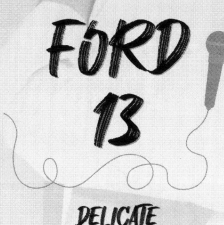

FORD

13

DELICATE

With a frustrated growl, I slam the door of the town car and survey my house. Today sucked. Millie was supposed to meet me for lunch, but she never showed. No text, no call. My daughter fucking ghosted me. I get it, of course. She's pissed about the pictures of Lake and me. But it still hurts.

According to Daniel, she refuses to talk about it even to him.

On my way up the steps, I loosen my tie, set on changing my mind-set. I only get three more nights with Lake before she leaves for Los Angeles.

When I open the door, my mood instantly lifts. The sight before me makes it impossible not to smile.

Lake in nothing but my blue dress shirt. All bare legs and wild hair, with her hips shaking as she sings along with the music in my kitchen. My black cat lying by her feet.

I undo the top button of my shirt and slip off my jacket. Without taking my eyes off her, I toss it aside. She's mesmerizing. Joy radiates off her as she holds the oversized spoon up to her lips like it's a mic.

As she spins and catches me watching, her lips tug up into a brilliant smile. "You're home!" She practically leaps into my arms and crushes me in a hug.

Pulling her as close as I can, I inhale her sweet vanilla scent. Everything about her is warm, welcoming. The way her body molds against mine, her excitement over seeing me. When was the last time anyone was genuinely happy to see me without getting anything in return? No handouts, no record deals. How long has it been since someone just wanted *me*?

I fist her hair and pull her face to mine, raking my fingers through her chocolate strands. "Hey, Red. Missed you today."

She kisses me lazily, tongue tangling with mine. Kissing just for the sake of kissing. My hands don't wander, and I don't want to let her go to take this any further. All I want is this connection.

Breathless, she pulls away and scans my face, then presses one last soft kiss against my lips. "Missed you too." She shimmies, silently signaling me to put her down. "But I had a great day." With her hand in mine, she pulls me toward the kitchen. "Sit. Let me open a bottle of wine."

In awe of her, I shake my head. She's completely comfortable in my house. She looks fucking good in my kitchen as well as in my shirt. "Let me get it."

I pad over to the bar and select a bottle I've been saving for a special occasion. Lake in my shirt, with no makeup on and her lips puffy from our kisses, was not what I originally had in mind for this thousand-dollar bottle of red, but I can't think of a more fitting reason if I tried. "What made your day so great?"

"Did you know that Nate and Amelia Pearson live in Bristol?"

Holding the corkscrew over the bottle, I pause and turn to her. Nate and Amelia aren't only famous for their music. Locally, they're known for being soulmates. "I didn't realize you knew them."

Her blue eyes are sparkling and her cheeks are flushed pink. "I saw Amelia perform at the Bluebird Café a few months before I had the chance to do it myself. She and Nate—they were the most adorable couple. So down to earth and so dedicated to one another despite the obstacles they had to overcome to make it." She shrugs. "They always gave me hope that one day I'd find that."

"Find what?"

Her eyes go soft and her shoulders lower just a fraction as she fixes her attention on the setting sun out the kitchen window. "True love. Finding that person who would choose me for me. Not for Lake Paige. But ya know just…me." She shuffles her bare feet on the tile and dips her chin. But after a silent moment, those blue eyes that are slowly making me believe I could maybe be that person for her find me. "You ever have that?"

I pull the cork out of the wine and turn to the cabinet to grab glasses. "True love?" I ask my reflection in the glass, too chicken to face her.

Her voice gets distant then. "You do have three children, so I don't know why I asked—"

"No," I say quickly as I turn around, holding two glasses.

Lake takes one step closer, then another, as I pour the wine. "No?"

I shake my head as I go to her, one glass held out. "Not like Nate and Amelia. Sure, I loved my ex at one time. But never in that *can't live without you* way. So no, I never had that before."

Lake takes the glass and nods, though she's focused on a spot on my throat rather than my face. "Me neither."

My damn heart picks up its pace and pounds against my sternum.

If she phrased the question differently, would I have the balls to give her an honest answer? Am I crazy for thinking that we could have that kind of love?

Is she wondering the same thing?

She's leaving in two days, and we still haven't discussed what will happen once she's gone. I'm not sure how to. Is this her way of broaching the subject?

"Ames wants to meet up at Thames on Friday. What do you think? I leave the next morning. Could be a fun last night together?"

She looks at me then, her eyes wide with excitement. I guess that's my answer. She's leaving on Saturday, and she isn't asking me to come with her or suggesting we figure out a way to continue what we've started. It ends after this.

"Why did you have a bad day?" she says, moving from one topic to the next with ease while I'm still in my head over what my life will look like when she's gone. When I'm back to coming home to an empty house. She's only been here for a few days. How is it possible that I can't imagine—or maybe don't *want to* imagine—this space without her?

"Just a bad day at work."

"Maybe I can make it better." She sets her glass of wine on the counter and takes mine as well. Then she pushes me toward the couch. I practically fall back onto the cushions when my calves make contact. Then she's straddling me. Our lips fuse together, and this time, I let my hands wander her body, kneading and massaging every inch of skin I can find.

When I get to her low back, I tease with one finger, then trace the line of her thong. I grip the full part of her ass and pull so her cheeks are spread. When she bucks in surprise, I bring my lips to her ear and tap the forbidden space. "Anyone ever had you here?"

She moans into my neck and breathes out a *no*.

"Good," I grunt. "I want to be the first. Will you do that for me, Lake? Let me have this virgin asshole? Let me make you feel good here too?"

I press gingerly, and she moans again, but then squirms as I push in further.

"Relax, Red. Not tonight. Tonight I just want this. You and me. A glass of wine. Dinner. Maybe the hot tub."

She licks her lips. "Will you dance with me too?"

"If you sing."

She smiles. "Always."

"But tomorrow," I rasp, "I want you to come to my office." The plan is already forming in my mind. If she's only mine until Saturday, then I don't want to spend a minute without her. And I want everything she'll give me.

She licks my lips. "Whatever you want, Mr. Hall."

My cock hardens at her teasing voice, and within seconds, she's helping me out of my pants and sinking down on top of me. Riding me. Kissing me. Fucking me like we have all the time in the world.

And fuck if I didn't wish we did.

LAKE
14

PAPER RINGS

W arm lips press against mine, but I force myself to keep my eyes shut.

"See you soon, Red," Ford whispers. A moment later, the bedroom door closes. When I hear the front door click shut, I bounce out of bed and rush to my suitcase.

The role play the other night got me thinking about how fun it would be to recreate another forbidden memory.

The day I signed with him.

Ford is objectively hot. I noticed that the moment I laid eyes on him. But back then, I was more enamored with the deal he'd proposed than by the way his almost silver eyes watched me. The hands I'm obsessed with now were only my focus for the moment it took him to sign the contract that gave me far too many millions and freedom from the assholes who were holding my music over my head.

Unlike my previous label, Ford's offer was for a partnership. The earnings for every album are split equally between me and the label. At the time, it was almost too good to be true and a blatant show of respect. One that forced me to block out any impure thoughts I might have had for the man. He was making all my dreams come true, and I refused to do anything that might jeopardize that.

Now my career is the last thing on my mind when I look at Ford. Although I've got lyrics and melodies floating through my head at all times. He stirs emotions in me that make no sense. We're nothing but a blip in time. Forbidden. Taboo. And yet somehow that makes us timeless.

For once, I'm not worrying about how another person feels about me or deconstructing where this will go.

I'm just living.

Feeling.

Wanting.

And what I want right now is to show up in Ford's office to reenact that meeting. But with a twist. I want to experience what could have happened if I'd seen him the way I see him now. If I'd been this desperate to seduce him back then. To feel his touch.

To live with reckless abandon. Without thought for anyone but the two of us.

THE OFFICE IS BUZZING the moment I walk in. Mouths fall open as I pass. Assistants and low-level execs flock to me, assuring me they can get me whatever I need. Phones in hands, no doubt recording my every step. It would all drain me if not for the man leaning against his office door. He's slipped back into his detached persona. It would be convincing if not for the hint of amusement tugging at those delicious lips.

Enjoying his scrutiny, I stop and sign every piece of paper that's thrust my way. I smile for every camera shoved in my face. Tilt my head and beam, knowing the entire world will soon discover that I'm visiting my ex-boyfriend's dad at his office today.

Knowing Paul will know.

God, why does that make my stomach flutter? There's got to be something seriously wrong with me, right? That I *like* the thought of him knowing I'm fucking his dad.

But I do, and from the flames in his father's eyes as he watches me saunter slowly toward him, he enjoys it too.

"Had to make a grand entrance, didn't you, Red?" He teases as he steps back to let me into his office.

Playing the part of an innocent, I bite my lip and give him a coy shrug.

Ford cuffs the back of my neck, his big palm warm against my skin, and pulls me back to the door, right where every one of his nosy employees can see. "Then give them a show," he taunts. His smirk tells me he knows precisely how wet he's making me by demanding I take what I want.

So I do just that. Feeling wicked, I pop up onto my toes and press my mouth to his. The kiss isn't chaste. No, I slide my tongue across his lips, forcing them to open, and then I revel in the deep, guttural groan I dig from his chest, clawing it out the way I claw at his shoulders to get better leverage on him.

When he pulls back, my red lipstick is smeared across his mouth. With a sharp exhale, he spins us and slams the door. He slaps a palm to the solid wood above my head and drops his forehead to mine. "Holy fuck." He lets out a raspy laugh that hits me right between the ribs.

"What did you want to talk to me about, Mr. Hall?" I pull back and affect the most demure, hesitant look I can manage.

Ford frowns at me, his forehead knotted in confusion.

"You asked me to come to your office. So is it safe to assume this has something to do with my music?"

His eyes flash then, like he's finally seeing the script I've just handed him. Sliding his hands into his pockets, he takes a step back and plays along. "Right. Take a seat, Lake. I'd like to discuss what's next for your tour."

God, he's so damn good at this. I finally unbutton my black jacket and let it fall open.

His eyes track the way it slides from my body, but he doesn't stop there. He continues his perusal down my bare legs and gets caught up on my short black skater skirt. Then a slow smile spreads across his face. Like he's trying his hardest to stay in character, he covers his mouth with his palm and schools his expression.

Without a word, he holds a hand out to the chair on this side of his desk, so I sit, crossing my legs and flexing my ankle, knowing the movement makes it hard for him to ignore all the skin on display.

To my surprise, he takes the seat behind his desk, making it difficult for me to really tease him. Just as he's settling, there's a knock on the door. My heart lurches at the sound, and I freeze. I want to yell that we're busy. I have a plan. But Ford, whose attention is now fixed on his laptop, wipes the lipstick from his face and hollers a "Come in," without even glancing at me.

A woman with deep auburn hair and a wide smile steps inside. She's decked out in a black dress that hugs her extraordinary curves. "Hey, darling," she drawls as she saunters across the office, ignoring me completely.

When she reaches Ford, she angles in close, shamelessly offering him more than a peek of her breasts. His eyes warm, though they don't dip down to her neckline, and he presses his lips to her cheek.

She palms his cheeks and scans his face, wearing a bright smile. "Been a long time, Ford. But somehow, you've only gotten prettier."

The deep chuckle that usually lights me up inside makes me stabby when it's aimed at another woman. I want those laugh lines, those sounds, that attention. It all belongs to me for another forty-eight hours, and at the moment, I'm irrationally possessive over them.

Ford shifts so he's facing me, and she follows his line of sight. "As much as I appreciate that," he says, holding a hand out, "the real prize is over there." He shakes his head at my expression, which is probably somewhere between *I'm going to murder this bitch* and *you're next on my list.*

My jealousy is so obvious I might as well have tossed gasoline around the room and threatened to throw a match.

The idea isn't terrible.

I want to set these feelings ablaze.

"I heard the rumors, but I figured that's all they were," the redhead says, adding fuel to the flames already licking up my insides.

I don't even know who this woman is, yet I'm ready to toss her out the window. What the hell is wrong with me? I'm *Lake fucking Paige. Act like it.*

"Lake, this is my old friend, Amanda. Mandy, I don't think Lake needs any introductions." The amusement in his expression has me settling a bit. She may think it's all rumors, but I know exactly what we are.

Fire.

An inferno so consuming I'm drawn to it. Entranced. I can't force myself away, no matter how much it burns. I want to feel every lick of his flame against every inch of my skin.

Fuck being burned. I want his scars.

"Ain't that the truth, hunny. It's a pleasure to meet you." She straightens and gives me a genuine smile.

"Mandy is the best tour manager in the business," Ford explains.

Finally, it hits me. In two days, I'm leaving for the next leg of my tour. I fired my tour manager in an epic way. For the last few shows, Ford took over those duties, but obviously, he can't follow me around the country.

That thought has me sitting back a little more in my chair, my bouncing leg suddenly motionless, my heart slowing.

Two more days.

And he's already preparing me for his departure from my life.

It shouldn't hurt. He's doing the mature thing, taking care of me when I'm clearly too reckless to care for myself. He's shown me more respect and affection and concern than any person I've slept with in the past. The rest of them have all left without a backward glance. Not a one has shown any concern for how I'll fare when they're gone.

I should appreciate that.

I don't.

"That's amazing." I force the Lake Paige smile to my lips. My voice is light and tinny in my own ears.

"She'll be taking over." He shifts in his seat, and worry flickers across his face for an instant, but it's gone before I can dissect its meaning. "You'll be in good hands."

Amanda wiggles her fingers in front of her. "The best!"

I jump up, because I was raised to offer handshakes when I'm introduced to someone new. For a minute there, I allowed my jealousy to overpower my manners. "I look forward to working together."

She rounds the desk, grinning at my outstretched hand, but when she steps in front of me, she pulls me in for a squishy hug. I practically bounce off her breasts with the force and have to stifle a surprised laugh. "In the south, we hug," she murmurs in my ear. When she pulls away, she turns to Ford. "How about I take Lake to lunch so we can discuss the next leg of the tour?"

Ford, who's got his elbows on his desk and his fingers steepled in front of him, nods silently.

With that simple move, the last of the breath he's been stealing from me over the last few days leaves my lungs in a final whoosh.

Disappointment swamps me as Ford stands. "We'll see you in an hour."

"Wait, what?" I spin and watch as he ushers her out the door and shuts it firmly behind her.

In the following silence, the click of the lock is deafening and his footsteps are thunderous.

Ford drops into his chair and leans back, his legs spread wide. "Come here, Red."

It takes effort to even breathe when he uses that tone.

On trembling legs, I move quickly. Two steps from him, I stop, waiting for his next command.

His face screws into an almost disappointed scowl. "What exactly are you wearing?" He tips forward and tugs on the hem of my skirt.

"Excuse me?" His demeanor has me twisting myself into a pretzel to decode his words and his expressions.

Ford grasps me behind the knees and rolls his chair across the hard-wood floor. His focus remains on my midsection as he drags his hands up the back of my thighs. When he reaches the swell of my ass, he tilts his head and pierces me with a look. The oxygen between us is snuffed out, leaving me dizzy as he works his fingers inward in slow caresses until he's pulling at my ass cheeks.

"No panties." He spits the words, his slate-blue eyes cooling to a gunmetal gray. "You came to a business meeting dressed like *this* with *no panties*?"

I suck in a breath and nod.

"I'm the only one who gets to see this bare cunt." He flips up the fabric of my skirt and drops his face to my center, inhaling my arousal.

Whimpers are the only sounds I'm capable of.

With a lick along my seam, he cranes his neck and rests his chin against my pelvis. "I could have scheduled meetings for you today. Another man could have seen *my* pussy, Lake. Is that what you wanted?" His hands are still kneading my ass, ramping up my pleasure.

"No. Sorry. That's not—this is only for you, Mr. Hall." My words are faltering, but my difficulty turns the cold gray of his irises molten.

"For me?" He regards me again, as if he's considering that thought, before he nudges his way between my legs and licks me like it's his job. Like he was born to drag my pleasure out for days, not to make me come, because he's not working me over hard enough for that. There's no sucking; just licking slowly, maybe for his own gratification.

"Yes, for you," I pant, grasping his hair and grinding my pelvis against his chin. I need friction, need him to give me more.

He pulls back, denying me. "Then bend over and show me you're mine."

"Fuck yes," I murmur, practically throwing myself on top of his desk.

Ford remains seated in his chair, spreading his legs wider and pulling me back so that my feet are touching the floor. In this position, my ass is in the air and my breasts are flattened against the papers on his desk. He crowds my space, his chest pressed against my back, and runs his fingers over the track pad on his laptop until an image of us appears on the screen.

"You're recording us?" I ask, my pulse skittering with a mix of fear and excitement.

A little red dot appears with a series of numbers beside it. "That a problem?"

Is it a problem? It should be. I should tell him to turn it off. Fucking my ex's father is one thing. A sex tape to go with it? That's insanity.

But the thought only adds to the slickness between my legs.

"Not a problem, sir."

The rumble of amusement that works its way up his chest sends a matching shudder up my spine. Gently, he presses a soft kiss against my hypersensitive skin and pushes my hair over one shoulder so there's no denying my identity.

I study the image. The woman who stares back is a stranger.

My face has been on every screen in America. Hundreds of billboards and thousands of magazine covers. Yet I don't recognize this woman at all. She's sexy and desperate. And with Ford clad in a suit, sitting behind me, I've been reduced to a puddle of need.

"Don't take your eyes off that screen, Red. I'm going to eat this pussy now."

He spreads me with both hands and then licks me once from front to back. With a groan, he spears me with his tongue. Then he alternates between sucking and licking while I can do nothing but babble incoherently.

I'm coming before I have a chance to take a full breath, arching and crying out for him.

"So fucking good," he murmurs as he sits up and looks into the camera, his eyes meeting mine through the screen. "I can't wait to have this ass."

"Yes. Please," I practically beg. Though I've come already, I need so much more. I need his cock to fill my every hole. I'm practically sobbing as I wiggle my ass, enticing him into moving quicker.

Ford licks between my cheeks, then uses a thumb to spread my wetness, toying with my clit, then dipping inside me before working his way back to my ass. Over and over, he does it, until I'm writhing and begging and boneless. When I'm thoroughly coated in my own arousal, he slowly fucks me with his finger.

"More," I beg.

Beside me, a drawer hisses open, then there's the sound of a condom wrapper being torn. Still pressed flat against his desk, I watch his movements on the screen. Watch as he unbuckles his belt and drops his pants to his ankles without care. His sole focus is on me as he gets ready to sheath himself. The goddamn smirk he directs at me makes my heart twist.

"I'm on birth control," I say quickly.

Ford pauses his movements and takes a heavy breath. "You want me to fuck you bare?"

"Y-yes," I stutter out. Then I meet his gaze, knowing he'll want me to demand it, not beg. "I want to feel every inch of you, Ford. No condom."

His lips twitch, but he stifles the smile that almost peeks out. "Still not giving you this cock in your ass, Red. Not yet. You need to be trained. Need to remember who you belong to before I give it to you."

His dirty words leave me writhing and racking my lust-addled brain for ways I can please him into fucking my ass. "I'll be good," I promise.

The loud slap registers before the bite of pain when his palm meets my ass. "You will, Red." He soothes my tender flesh. "You're gonna be good for me and take my bare cock in this cunt. You're gonna be dripping for me and begging for it until tonight. Then, maybe if you make me proud, I'll fuck this tight little virgin ass. You want that?"

I nod against the desk. "Yes. Please fuck me. Please." I rock back, desperate to be closer, but Ford holds me in place with one hand on my hip. Then he presses inside me with a curse, and the heat of him without the barrier of a condom breaks me. "So fucking good, Red. So warm, so fucking perfect. The best I've ever had."

That confession only makes me more eager. I'm a competitive person by nature, so the praise is like catnip. It leaves me wanting to give him more.

He thrusts until he's fully seated, then angles over me and presses a kiss to my shoulder. "I'll never get enough of you." His words are gentle and so quiet it's unlikely the microphone picked them up. This is just for me. For us.

"Are you ready, baby?"

When I nod, he pulls back, then slams into me. He does it again and again, picking up the pace until his thrusts are brutal. Exactly how I like them. I'm clenching down on him as he hits my G-spot over and over. Then I shatter a thousand times, our sounds and murmured words a blur lost in the abyss of ecstasy.

Without slowing, he leans to one side and pulls something from his desk drawer. Then he's groaning and coming in hot spurts, pulsing aftershocks from my own orgasm teasing us both. I'm just about bone-less when he pulls out and slides a finger inside me. I shudder on contact, overly sensitive, but relax again as he withdraws and drags the mixture of his release and mine to my ass and fingers me slowly again.

"Take a deep breath, baby," he warns, his expression tender on screen.

I obey, pulling in a lungful of air. As I release it, I feel the pinch of cool metal pressing inside. He hums in approval as he stares at the object he just put there.

Surprisingly, it doesn't hurt. Just a bit of pressure.

"Fuck, Red, I can't tell you how good you look wearing a diamond in your ass."

FORD
15

LAVENDER HAZE

Every time Lake shifts in her seat, my cock twitches. With each move, she's feeling another punch of the anal plug. I certainly didn't see myself buying her a diamond when this started, but fuck if I'm not annoyed now that this is the only kind I can ever give her.

She let me take her completely bare, and I'm still reeling. Nothing in this world has ever felt better. And I can't wait to do it again.

"She won't disappear if you look away," Gavin teases.

Beside him, Beckett tries and fails to stifle a grin.

"You don't look away from perfection, boys."

"Perfection would be your son coming to play hockey for me before the end of this season." Gavin's retort hits at the exact moment Daniel steps into the box.

Fortunately he doesn't hear him, but the kid instantly staggers when he spots Lake. She's by the bar, surrounded by a small crowd. Right now, she's talking to Olivia Maxwell, the woman who runs PR for Beckett and Gavin. By the way Beckett tracks her every move, it's clear she means a lot more to him than he wants to let on.

With a nod to the guys, I head for my son and pull him in for a hug.

When he steps out of my embrace, he's grinning. "Hey, Dad."

"Thanks for coming. Hit any traffic?"

"Nah." Daniel shakes his head. "Sorry I'm late. I was trying to convince Millie to come. Now that I'm here, though, I realize it's probably better she skipped." He juts his chin in Lake's direction. "So what they're saying is true?"

I don't know how to answer the question. What I have with Lake is the truest thing I've experienced outside of parenting. Outside of my relationships with my kids, life is nothing but superficial. Fame and money and prestige. And now, with the twins so close to finishing college and living their own lives, the number of real things left is dwindling.

"Yes." I keep my response simple. I've always strived to remain transparent with my kids.

"Millie will come around eventually. If you have real feelings for one another—"

I hold my hand up to put a stop to this conversation. "Her tour picks back up this weekend. Just watch the game and don't worry about it. Don't worry about your sister either. I'll work things out with her."

The people around us erupt into cheers, spurring us to turn our attention to the ice where Aiden Langfield is on a breakaway toward New York's net. The goalie is braced as he waits to see which way Aiden will go, but in the end, he can't stop the biscuit from sliding into the back left corner. The crowd in the box goes wild as Aiden punches the air in celebration.

"Ya know Mikey got called up to Arizona?" The way Daniel eyes the ice is reminiscent of the way Beckett was just looking at his head of PR. Shit. Is that what I look like when I can't pull my focus from Lake?

Regardless, in this moment two things become clear to me. One, I'm going to let my son join the team this season if it's what he really wants, and two, it's going to be impossible to watch Lake walk away.

"DID you see how cool her hair was?" Lake hasn't stopped talking since we left the game. Daniel, thank fuck, treated her like normal. He promised to make time to have lunch with her when her tour stopped in Florida, and she promised to leave tickets at will-call for his buddies.

"It was very interesting."

Gavin offered to buy a woman a drink at the bar where we all ended up after the game. What the idiot didn't realize was that he'd slept with her before.

In his defense, once he figured out who she was, he swore her hair used to be blonde. Now it was jet-black and cut just above her chin, with ragged edges that almost looked like spikes.

Beside me in the back of the SUV, Lake twirls the ends of her hair. "It was so unique. So different from the way I've always worn mine."

I press closer to her, dropping a kiss against the soft skin of her neck. "If you like the style, why not try it out for yourself?"

Beneath me, she freezes. "Right. Because you'd ever allow me to do that."

Her words are like being hit by a snowball when I had no idea there'd even been a storm.

"I don't *allow* you to do anything. You're your own person, Lake."

She pulls back, her face scrunched up in disbelief. I don't like the look one bit. "*Please.* Like the label would ever let Ms. Perfect destroy her famous long locks."

Anger coils tighter inside me, making every muscle tense. "Neither I nor the label control you, Lake."

She scoffs like she doesn't believe me and ducks her chin.

I pull her closer, running my hand behind her neck and fisting her hair at her scalp so she's forced to look at me, making sure she understands my every word. "I don't give a fuck about your reputation. And I definitely have no say in how you do your hair. So long as there is enough of *this* to grab while you're on your knees, I'm fine."

She lets out a surprised yelp as I tug on her hair, her red lips parting. "You're not serious."

I yank harder, forcing her head back and exposing her neck, giving me the perfect place to lick. "As a heart attack. You don't need anyone's permission, Red. You're in control. Now tell me what the fuck you want me to do to you right now."

She glances at the partition, worrying her lip.

Squeezing her thigh, I angle in close and nip at her ear. "Anders is not going to open the door or stop the car until I tell him to. So tell me, what do you want?"

"Your cock in my mouth," she whispers. Her swallow is heavy, like she's confessing a sin.

"Tell me, then, with my diamond in your ass and my cock down your throat, what the fuck are we going to do about that pussy?"

"It's going to be soaked for you, Ford. *Drenched.*"

"Good girl," I murmur, licking a line up her neck. My cock is rock hard at just the taste of her. "On your knees, Red. Palms on *my* knees. You're gonna let me fuck that throat until you're writhing and begging me to fill that ass, isn't that right, baby?"

She lets out a breathy moan and scrambles to the floor of the SUV. Her Bolts jersey and black leather pants make it impossible to see her body's reaction, but I'll lick her clean later.

Once I unbuckle my pants, she practically leaps at me, trying to get her hands on my dick.

Voice low, I chide her impatience. "Where are your hands supposed to be?"

She sucks in a surprised breath and brings her wide eyes to mine, but a heartbeat later, she scrambles into place.

"Good girl," I murmur again, caressing her cheek with my thumb. "Now open those red lips for me."

Her mouth drops open at my command, sending pleasure worming its way straight to my cock. She's so fucking obedient. I love it as much as I hate it. Because it makes me want to keep her. Makes me want to protect her. No one else will take the kind of control she offers and hand it right back to her. Other men will abuse the power she gives so freely.

All I want to do is use it for her pleasure.

She licks at her lips and whines, impatient, desperate for me to move forward, desperate for my cock.

The sound, the way she practically begs for me to destroy her, makes my knees weak.

Thank fuck I'm sitting down.

I cover the slip in control with a chuckle. "Look at you. All of America thinks you're the sweetheart. Ms. Perfect. But we both know better. You're dying for my cock right now, aren't you?"

Blue eyes shining, she sticks her tongue out and waits.

Fisting my length, I close my eyes, bracing myself for her mouth. I have to make this last. We've got less than forty-eight hours left together, and I intend to fuck her for most of them. I tangle the fingers of my free hand in her hair and pull her to my waiting dick. She moves eagerly, lips parting wider, then I'm pushing inside her warm mouth slowly.

"Fuck, Red. You are the most perfect thing that ever existed. No one has ever made me feel this fucking good."

She hums in response, lips tipping up around my cock and eyes watering.

I thrust forward again, and I'm rewarded with a sigh. Like she's loving every second of giving me control. The car lurches forward then, jostling us, and she gags as I hit the back of her throat. "You okay?"

Closing her eyes, she inhales deeply through her nose, but she doesn't pull away. When she looks at me again, blue irises glittering, my chest suddenly feels too tight. She's too far away, even as she consumes me like this. I need her like I need my next breath. Hands shaking, I release her hair and scoop her off the floor. I pull her onto my lap and devour her. Hands on her cheeks and mouth melded to hers.

"Ford." The word is like a prayer on her lips.

We both need more, and I'm beginning to think I'll never get enough.

"I know, baby." I pour every part of me into her. Words can't describe what exists in the space between us. I'm not sure our bodies could even express it adequately, though I'll damn well try my hardest to get us there. With my heart pounding out a rapid beat against hers, I hold her close and clear my throat. "Anders," I call out, "we're ready when you are."

He's been driving in circles, waiting for my direction, but it only takes a couple of minutes before we come to a stop. When he knocks on the door, Lake and I have already adjusted our clothing, and I've smoothed her hair back. I help her out of the car, and because she's Lake, she offers Anders a shy smile and a quiet thank-you and good night.

I don't bother with niceties, though. My cock is painfully aware of what's about to happen, and my only focus is on getting Lake into my bed now.

Once we're inside, I forgo the lights. In the dark, I scoop her up and carry her up the stairs and to my bedroom.

Lake nuzzles into my chest and lets out a content sigh. The sound only fuels my desire. I want all her sounds. All her joy. All her moments.

Her.

It's impossible to ignore just how much.

"Get undressed. I want you completely bare. No heels. Nothing but you." I press a gentle kiss to her forehead before setting her on her feet on the plush rug. Then I head to the bathroom, in search of supplies.

When I return, she's standing in front of my bed, bathed in the moonlight, completely nude and absolutely breathtaking. She raises her chin, and a bit of nervousness slips through, as evidenced by the trembles that skitter across her chest.

I yank back the comforter and toss the supplies onto the bed, and in two strides, I'm in front of her, touching her, warming her. "There's nothing to be scared of. You know I won't ever hurt you, right?"

I study her, watching for even the tiniest reaction. The moment her shoulders relax and the furrow between her brow disappears, my heart skips a beat. Fuck, I'm so screwed.

Settling my palm against her hip, I pull her in and fuse my mouth with hers. The kiss is slow, timeless. It has no purpose other than to bring us closer. Without breaking apart, we stumble to the bed. I give her arms a gentle push, and when she falls onto the mattress, I hum in appreciation. Fuck, does she look incredible in my bed.

"You are wearing far too many clothes," she says, teasing tone back in place. The sound sends a ripple of excitement up my spine.

Slowly, without looking away, I strip for her. One piece of clothing at a time, exaggerating all my movements. The bemused smirk she wears as she watches only builds the tension between us until my cock is straining for her, weeping, waiting for the moment we've promised since this morning.

"Hold your knees wide open for me, Red. I want to see what sucking my cock did to you."

She obeys, splaying her hands on her thighs and pressing them apart. Her head lolls to the side and her chest heaves under my examination. She's glistening and pink, just as I suspected. I sweep the pile of supplies to one side of the bed, then drop to my own knees and pull her to the edge of the mattress.

"How's your ass feel?" I ask, running my nose along the crease of her thigh, inhaling her aroused scent.

She sighs out a "ready."

Licking between her pussy lips, I confirm just how true that statement is. "Need you to come first, then you'll really be ready." I don't wait for her to agree. I just get to work, lapping at her and teasing her clit. Pride swells in my chest as I do. Because though it's only been a few days, I know just how to kiss this pussy and precisely what she needs.

She writhes and fists the sheets, moaning and begging for release. "Please, Ford. Please."

Her chants have me spreading her ass cheeks and releasing the diamond bead, all while I work her pussy until she's screaming for me just like I want. She tastes so fucking good, so sweet. The moment I work my finger into her ass, spreading her wider, letting her smooth hole suck me in, she surprises me.

Fuck.

As if this moment couldn't get any better, she squirts.

"Holy shit," she rasps, bowing off the bed.

In response, I lick up every drop, fucking thrilled that she's covered my tongue.

"Did I just—"

"Come all over my face? Yes you did, baby. Yes you fucking did." I crawl on top of her and kiss her so she knows just how incredibly hot that moment was. I won't give her a second to doubt it or feel an ounce of shame. "I'm going to fuck your ass now."

Lake nods, her brow furrowed. She's so serious and determined as she studies my face.

Without looking away, I pat the mattress until I find the bottle of lube. "Turn over, baby." I raise myself up onto my knees and sheath myself while she gets situated with a pillow under her belly and her ass in the air. I give the masterpiece a gentle tap, and she wiggles it. "Are you nervous?" I ask, pressing closer and squirting a generous dollop of lube onto my fingers.

As I press against her ass, she flinches. I rest my other palm on her side and stroke her slowly, waiting for her to relax.

"I'm just—" She peers over her shoulder at me. "You have a really big cock."

I let out a pleased laugh. "You can take it, Red. I believe in you."

She giggles. "This isn't like going out on stage, Ford. You have no idea what it feels like to have a huge cock shoved up your ass. Or do you?" Another giggle.

I laugh as I work two lubricated fingers inside her. "No, I definitely do not. But I know there isn't a person on this planet who works harder than you, so if anyone can handle this…"

A soft smile covers her face and grows until it reaches her eyes.

"Grab the wand," I instruct, nodding to the device beside her.

Her mouth forms an O when she catches sight of it, like she hadn't noticed its presence until now.

"Turn it on and play with your clit, baby. I'm going to fuck you now."

She takes a deep breath, but like the good girl she always is, she complies, teasing herself with it like I asked.

Scooting closer, I push into her pussy first, giving her a few pumps.

Shit. I have to squeeze my eyes shut and clench my ass cheeks as I do. Watching her like this, feeling her warmth suck me in, has me too close to coming. She grinds against me as I pull out, chasing her pleasure. With one more squirt of lube, I massage my dick, then drag the head up and press it to her ass. "Take a deep breath," I warn, and when she does, I push in.

She cries out as she clamps down on me.

I grab her hips and hold the both of us still. "Breathe, baby."

Obediently, she takes a haggard breath. "Okay."

"Good girl. Keep that wand on your clit," I whisper, running a palm across her ass, soothing her as I push in another inch.

The farther I go, the more she relaxes, but her whines only escalate. "Does it hurt?"

She shakes her head, rubbing her face along the sheets. "No, just… keep going."

I slide in another inch, thrusting gently, and do it again until my hips are flush against her. When I hold there, we let out matching sighs. "How does it feel?" I ask, digging my fingers into her hips.

The buzzing from the wand is deafening. The only thing that would make this moment better is if I could see the way she's working her clit with it. Definitely should have recorded this too.

"So good," she whines. "For you?"

The pleasure coiling in my stomach is so acute I have to squeeze my eyes shut again. Fuck, her ass squeezes me tighter as she writhes on her toy.

"Can barely breathe because I don't want to miss a minute," I grit out. "Can I move now?"

At her nod of permission, I pull back almost as slowly as I entered, then I thrust back in, causing a yelp to pass those perfect lips.

"Oh my god. I think I'm going to come again."

"Good, you better drench those sheets, baby." Gritting my teeth, I thrust again, ramping up my pace, and in seconds, my balls are so tight I'm on the precipice of my own orgasm. There's no way I'll finish without getting her off once more, so I double down on my efforts. Her spasms intensify, making it impossible to hold out any longer. Thank fuck. Just as I lose control, she cries out that she's coming. I hold her in place as I empty inside her, pleasure nearly causing me to black out.

It feels like a lifetime passes before my vision clears and my lungs fill with oxygen. When I come back to myself, I slide out of her, take care of the condom, and wet a washcloth in the bathroom. The room is dim, the only light coming from the lamp on one nightstand as I clean her up. The sight of her languid body and the sounds she makes have me desperate to please her again. So I flip her to her back and get to work cleaning up her front, this time with my tongue. I take my time licking her cum from her now swollen lips until she comes again, shouting incoherently as she does.

After she begs me to stop, I curl up next to her and pull her close, threading my fingers through her hair. More than any other moment we've shared today, this is the one I'll remember when she's gone. Her warm body in my arms, the way she trusts me to care for her, and how it feels like she's holding on just as tightly, wishing that tonight would never end.

LAKE
16

WILDEST DREAMS

I wake up with Ford between my legs. Again. It should be criminal to experience this much pleasure in one week.

"You're spoiling me," I rasp, though instead of fighting it, I rake my hands through his hair and hold him in place until I'm shaking.

When I go limp, he pulls me on top of him and forces me to ride him until we're both sweaty messes and exhausted again. "We should stay in bed all day," Ford suggests, stroking my back as I lie on his chest, listening to the rhythm of his heart.

"You're not going to work?"

With a soft smile, he cups my chin. "Not a chance. Play hooky with me today?"

The smile that splits my face is so big my cheeks ache. "Can we go to breakfast? And maybe go for a walk downtown?"

One last day to be Lake and Ford. Not Lake Paige, who has to go back to her real life and put on a show again, day after day. And not just on a stage, but in the production I've realized my life is. Constantly being on. Constantly smiling. Not because I feel actual joy, but because I *should* feel joy. Because I *should* appreciate all I have when, for so long, it was all I wanted. My career, my fans, my fame.

Only it's not what I want anymore. More than anything, I want to be a girl in a small town who is loved by this man.

Even if we have an expiration date. Even if it's not real. For today, I'd like to pretend I'm his entire world. Because it's clear to me now that if we didn't have a time limit, he'd become mine.

With his lips against mine, Ford murmurs, "We can do anything you want, Red. Today's all about you."

"And you," I reply, leaning in and kissing him.

"That's good news for you, because I just want to be wherever you are. So you lead and I'll follow."

The words light a small fire in my chest that warms me from the inside out. With a soft sigh, I snuggle him again. I really could get used to this.

WE SPEND the day popping into one store after another, hands clasped and smiles easy. Ford bought every single item I commented on. The first time he pulled out his wallet, I argued. I don't really need the bangle engraved with the town's coordinates.

He slipped it around my wrist anyway and held it there, gaze heavy. "Please, Red," he whispered, "let me give you something to remember me by."

I wanted to tell him that I had no intention of forgetting him. God, I couldn't if I tried. If only I could get the words out. Garner my strength and tell him that there'd be no need to forget him if we just keep doing what we're doing.

Being happy, making love.

But because I'm a coward, I accepted the bracelet and every other thing he purchased. Sunglasses, a new hat, a pair of glittery earrings, and a blue cashmere scarf. He tugged it around my neck and kissed me. "It's the color of my eyes," he said.

We both knew it was a replacement for the red one I'd continued to wear to keep warm. I tossed the old scarf into the trash as we walked out of the store.

That evening, we had dinner in a tiny Italian restaurant, and Ford told me all about the first record he produced. It was wild hearing about his side of the business I knew so well. I soaked up every detail. Stories about the early days of his career. Where he started. How much he'd accomplished. Each new fact only made me appreciate him more.

As he guides me into Thames now, his arm looped firmly around my waist, I can feel the clock ticking down on our time together.

"Maybe we should just go home," I choke out, cursing the way my heart cracks.

He pulls me closer but keeps pushing forward. "Let's do what we both love, baby. Let's listen to some music."

I heave a sigh but don't argue. It's probably for the best. It's going to be impossible to walk away from this man. No amount of time in his bed will change that. At least here, I can focus on the music rather than on the little time we have left.

Nate wanders over when he spots us, and he and Ford exchange pleasant hellos before he pulls me in for a warm hug. "Ames is just checking on the baby," he says, pointing to the ceiling. "Her best friend owns this place. Normally Ames stays home with our Paulie girl on Fridays, but she wanted to see you, so the baby is napping in the apartment upstairs."

"I'm glad I get to see you both. It really takes me back."

Nate tips his head back and laughs. "God, I wouldn't go back to those times if you paid me."

Jaw dropping, I rear back and try to decipher his expression.

He waves his hand in jest. "Not that it wasn't great. It's just—" His eyes flit to one side and lock on something over my shoulder. Ford and I both turn and find Amelia sauntering toward us. She literally stole her husband's breath.

The tall blonde who rarely smiles presses a kiss to her husband's jaw before she even greets us. At the sight of their easy love, I have to swallow back my envy.

"What was I saying?" Nate asks with a big grin on his face.

"I think what you were saying is that you prefer married life to playing in bars by yourself," Ford suggests rather astutely.

Amelia shakes her head as she laughs. "Always so swoony, Nate Pearson. But you know you're gonna get lucky tonight. No need to sweet-talk me."

Nate's only response is a wicked smile directed at his wife.

My heart is cracking in my chest as Ford's eyes meet mine. The expression on his face tells me he sees what I see.

That's real love. That's *it*. The thing people write songs about. The reason stadiums sell out. We're all chasing that feeling. No wonder these two haven't gone on tour. There's nothing to chase. They have it all right here in this little bar on the water in their hometown. With their child sleeping upstairs and a guitar leaning against the fireplace, just waiting for Nate to pick it up and play. What more could they need?

"You ready for some music?" Amelia asks, pulling up a chair and setting it beside me.

"You going to play?" Ford asks her.

She shrugs. "I'm sure Nate and I will get a set in. Maybe you want to join?" Her brows are lifted and her expression is bright as she focuses on me.

I shake my head. Tonight is about watching. Learning. God, could I use a few lessons, and not all of them are about music. "I'm excited to be a fan tonight."

She shrugs. "Suit yourself. I'm going to see if Hailey needs help at the bar. Be back in a bit."

The first artist to take the tiny stage has a voice like Jewel, all gravel and gorgeous. I'm immediately lost in the moment. The guy who follows doesn't have quite as much talent, but he can work the crowd like none other.

Then Nate grabs his guitar, pulls his hat backward and sits on the lone stool. A hush takes over the room as he gets situated. It lasts so long I start to fidget, but I freeze again when Amelia's rasp fills the room. It's a cappella and angelic, and from the adoring expression on her husband's face as he watches her, she's utterly captivated him. She takes slow steps, one after another, from the bar to the stage. His fingers don't start strumming until she's at his side.

"Holy shit," I mutter under my breath when they finish their set.

Ford nods beside me. "It's been a while since I sat in a bar and scouted out talent, but *fuck*. If they didn't already have a deal, I'd offer them one right here."

"You miss this part of it?" I ask, resting a hand on his bicep.

He dips his chin. "Didn't realize how much until now." He takes a sip of his whiskey, and then his eyes find mine. "You know, I saw you at the Bluebird many years ago."

My breath catches, and I sit a little straighter. "You did?"

He brings his lowball to his lips again and hums. "You were incredible. I was there to meet with someone else, but I left thinking only of you."

"But you didn't approach me until years later," I remind him, my stomach sinking just a little.

"You were picked up the next day. The deal happened too quickly. I shoulda signed you on the spot. Big mistake," he mutters.

"Huge!" I retort with a grin, mimicking *Pretty Woman*.

His responding laugh and the lightness in his eyes make my heart jump. "But I still got you. Honestly, nothing was a bigger mistake than not asking you out before Paul did."

This time my lungs seize in my chest and I rear back. "What?"

Scrubbing a hand over his face, he huffs. "Fuck, Lake. Life would have been so different if I'd just gone for it when I saw you again two years ago."

"You think not asking me on a date is a bigger miss than not signing me?" My pulse flutters at the intense way he's watching me. "Seriously? We've made millions together."

He doesn't hesitate. "I'd rather have you." His grip on my hand is tight, unyielding, his focus clear. *All on me.*

My throat clogs, and I have to look away. If he had, then maybe what we have could be real. It could have worked. The thing I witnessed between Nate and Amelia, that forever, soulmate kind of love, that's what I feel when I'm in this man's presence. He could have been it for me.

But he didn't take that chance, and now we're nothing but a news story. Lake Paige gets revenge with her ex-boyfriend's dad. We've made a mockery of what we could have been.

WE DON'T STICK around another minute. Quickly waving goodbye, we head out into the night, silent. There's simultaneously so many unspoken words between us and nothing left to be said.

The second we step through the door to his house, we're attacking one another. We peel away our clothing, layer by layer, our movements in sync until Ford lays me down and covers me with his hard body. He warms me from the inside out as he sinks inside one last time, moving slowly, never breaking eye contact. The experience is haunting and beautiful and soul shattering. Desperate to leave my mark on him, wishing there was a way I could physically become a part of him, I dig my nails into his back.

When we come together, tears stream down my face, but still, we say nothing. We simply kiss one another through it. He knows why I'm crying. I don't want it to be over. But because he can't change our circumstance, he doesn't even try to stop the tears.

"If he wasn't my son—" The sound of his voice in the quiet startles me from my thoughts. It's the vulnerability in his tone. The yearning. His stormy eyes are a beacon guiding me to his truth.

I nuzzle into his neck, silently assuring him that he doesn't need to finish that thought. I know his heart. It's stamped on mine. The feel of his hands against me are the safety net I never knew I needed. His tone, his demeanor, all of it tells me all the things I need to know. Everything I've ever wanted to hear.

He swallows thickly, his Adam's apple bobbing against me. The movement forces the knot in my chest to tighten and press against my lungs so forcefully it's hard to take in air. Disappointment consumes me. He can be nothing more than the man who put me back together after my heart had been broken by his son. Though not a single moment with Paul was as powerful as the one I'm living with Ford now. Outside of the relationship between the two men, I haven't thought of Paul at all. I haven't missed him a bit.

I don't beg Ford to choose me. I don't speak at all. Instead, I respond by pressing closer to his body and fusing our lips. When the first hints of daylight stream into his bedroom, I take a moment to memorize every inch of his face, and while his eyes are still closed, I disappear from his life.

FORD
17

DAYLIGHT

Before I even opened my eyes, I knew she was gone. It made her either the biggest coward or the bravest person I know. I certainly couldn't have walked away if she'd asked me to. Couldn't have watched her leave either.

I simultaneously hate her for it and appreciate the hell out of her for not making me.

The house is unbearably quiet without her, and I don't even have work to distract me. Not that I'll let that deter me from heading into Boston. I'd have the office to myself on a Saturday morning and I can't bear to stay home.

It's rare that I have a free day, yet it is the last thing I want when she isn't here with me. There is no one to dance around the kitchen with or slip into the hot tub beside. No one to share a meal with or cuddle up to beneath the covers.

And if I couldn't have her, then there never would be.

I'd given up believing there was a person out there who could be all mine. I'd had my children, I'd done that dance, and I'd bowed out during the second act. I didn't deserve to try again. Especially not with someone who had all those milestones in front of her. She deserved marriage, a honeymoon phase, and kids if she wanted them. She deserved everything and then some. I was on the sunset of all of that. Looking back at the day and appreciating all I'd been given. All the experiences I'd had. She was just waking up and stretching her arms.

I make it eight hours without reaching out. I know she landed in Los Angeles because Amanda sent me an update. The two of them were meeting for a late dinner to go over tour details, so I have no excuse to contact her. I know she's safe, but I send the text anyway.

> Ford: Get home safe?

The dots bounce on the screen for so long I nearly shout in frustration and consider throwing my phone across the room. Buttons meows and pushes her way under my arm, and for a moment, I settle. Then the phone beeps loudly with her response, and I'm hit with a mix of anticipation and apprehension.

> Lake: Yup. Thank you for showing me around your town and introducing me to your friends. They are all wonderful and I really enjoyed myself.

I read the message over and over, and then I really do throw the phone. When it clatters to the ground, I hope to fuck the screen is cracked so I never have to see that goddamn polite bullshit again.

She appreciates being shown around my town and she likes my friends? How about all the orgasms I gave her? The fucking love we made? Does she intend to send a thank-you basket for those too? Knowing her, the answer is probably yes. Fuck.

She'd probably send chocolates as an expression of gratitude for helping her get through her breakup.

Fuck, I'm pissed.

I wait six hours before I text her again.

> Ford: Don't thank me. You gave me the best week of my life, Red. If you take one thing from our time together, please let it be that. You're in charge. You call the shots. Demand what you want and take it. You've fucking earned it.

> Lake: It was the best week of my life, too.

WEDNESDAY NIGHT, Daniel meets me just inside the main doors at Bolts Arena, but his sister is absent again. "Sorry, Dad, I tried."

Disappointment hangs between us. I haven't heard from Paul, but I know he's fine anyway. The paps are still snapping photos of him on his stupid luxury vacation. Looks like Clay is paying his way now.

I expected anger from him, yet I never got it. And while I knew Millie and Daniel would be affected and may have questions or concerns, I had no idea she'd take it this hard. If I had, would I have made different choices? Would I have chosen to miss out on experiencing Lake the way I did?

No. My daughter means the world to me, but eventually, she'll learn that none of us are perfect. We love who we love.

Not that I'll ever get to say that to the woman who owns my heart.

Maybe that's the issue. Millie and I have yet to speak about Lake. Does she believe what she's read? If so, then she probably thinks I'm nothing but a scumbag who had an affair with my son's ex. But since my daughter was born, I've been her biggest supporter, her person—maybe more than even her twin. We've always been exceptionally close. She should know I wouldn't have done what I did if Lake didn't mean something to me. She should know that's not who I am.

We wander through the empty corridor and down the tunnel that leads to the ice. The team isn't playing today, and Daniel knows that.

I'm sure he follows their schedule much like anyone who has an obsession.

It took being consumed by my own obsession to realize precisely what I needed to do. I reminded Lake over and over that she was in control of her life, but I'd kept my son on a tight leash, tethering him to my expectations rather than allowing him the opportunity to make his own choices.

We find Gavin standing by the ice, his head bowed and his thumbs moving furiously over the screen of his phone. He shakes his head and lets out a loud laugh that echoes through the empty rink.

"Let me guess," I say, approaching. "Your brother?"

Gavin turns his big smile on us. "I swear the Langfield brother group chats could get us all fired."

Daniel stands beside me, frowning and looking from Gavin to me and back again. He hasn't asked about why I invited him to meet me here, but now he's clearly curious.

Gavin pockets his phone and lifts one brow in silent question. With a nod, I take a step back. This isn't my moment. Daniel deserves to hear this straight from the person who's about to offer everything he's spent his life working for.

With a hand outstretched, Gavin greets my son. "We're having one hell of a season, don't you think?"

Daniel shakes his hand and glances at me again, his brow furrowed in confusion. But there, mixed in with his puzzlement, is a hint of hope and maybe a little disbelief. "The team looks great, sir."

"I've got to be honest, though. I think we're missing something." Gavin puts his hands in his pockets and turns toward the ice. As if on cue, the team exits the locker room, their loud voices and chatter filling the empty rink.

Brooks Langfield, the star goalie, oversized in both height and personality, approaches first. He points at Gavin and shakes his head. "Mom is going to lose her shit."

Gavin simply lifts a brow and shrugs.

Aiden's next, the center who's sure to be a hall-of-famer if his stats continue their upward trajectory. "Forget Mom. Beckett is going to string him up by the balls."

Tyler Warren—War to his teammates and fans—the right winger and well-known instigator, laughs as he steps onto the ice. "Epic, man. Totally fucking epic!"

"What the fuck are you all going on about?" Rowan Parker, the defenseman, asks as he skates in circles nearby.

Gavin sports a cocky grin, affecting the cool demeanor of a younger brother who's definitely involved in something that'll piss off his older one. "ESPN asked if they could have the event here. All I did was tell them that Beckett would prefer to host them at the stadium."

Aiden lets out a high-pitched squeal. "And then you didn't tell him it was for the swimsuit edition. Guy is livid."

"All right, enough gossiping," the coach says as he wanders over. "You get them all worked up, and then tonight they'll be like fucking teenage girls hopped up on candy."

Beside me, Daniel's mouth is ajar and his eyes are full of stars. He's surrounded by all of his idols, and every last one of them is joking around.

"Speaking of players," Gavin says, hollering over the chatter around us. "I'd like to introduce you all to Daniel Hall."

My son's swallow is audible as every head turns in his direction.

"We were wondering if you'd like to suit up with the guys and skate a bit," Gavin offers nonchalantly.

With all eyes on him, Daniel blinks at me. "Is this for real?" he mutters.

"It's your decision. Though I expect that you'll finish that degree."

He's nodding before I can get the final word out. Then the coach is draping an arm over his shoulder and ushering him toward the locker room. I watch on as my son starts on a journey that he's waited his whole life for, feeling nothing but pride and excitement for him.

Gavin steps up beside me and nudges my shoulder. "What made you change your mind?"

"Just realized that he deserved the choice. It's not mine to make for him."

With a hum, he rocks on his heels. "Kind of like allowing a woman to decide whether she wants to be with you? To come to her own decision about what makes her happy, rather than taking it upon yourself to decide that she deserves better?" His focus remains fixed on his players, who are now in full-on practice mode, but his question hits like a dagger straight to my heart anyway.

"It's not the same."

"Why?" This time he does turn to me, his gaze boring into my face.

I'm too chickenshit to look him in the eye when I reply. "Because she does deserve better. As do my kids."

Gavin snorts. "Paul is having a grand ole time in Bali, so that's bullshit."

Gritting my teeth, I finally turn to my jackass friend, but he goes on before I can argue.

"And you just gave Daniel everything he's ever wanted. So is this about Millie, or is this about you being afraid to ask Lake if you're enough?"

"Millie will never accept us."

Clasping my shoulder, he gives it a good squeeze. "I say this with all the respect in the world, man, but your daughter is a spoiled brat if she can't see past the image the media portrays. She knows you, and she knows your heart. She'll figure it out." He purses his lips and gives me a once-over before he goes on. "You've given her everything she's ever wanted. Maybe now it's time to take a little bit for yourself. In a few years, when Mills meets someone, do you really think she's going to take your feelings into consideration?"

All of it makes my chest tight. Fuck. I let out a long sigh in hopes of relieving the discomfort. The idea of my baby girl giving herself to anyone makes me a bit sick, to be honest. But Gavin's not exactly wrong. She's not even talking to me now. When I leave here, I'll go home to an empty house again. And though she's surrounded by people, Lake is all alone too.

And just the thought of anyone else laying a hand on her instantly sparks a rage so fierce inside me it's almost uncontrollable. She asked if I'd ever been in love. The kind people write songs about, and I lied through my teeth.

I told her every guy she'd ever dated was an idiot, but I'm the biggest one of all. I pull out my phone and do some math before turning to my friend again. "You'll let Daniel know I had to go?"

The smirk on Gavin's face is all ego. "Depends on where you're going."

I'm already moving before I reply. "Going to bring a girl some ice cream."

LAKE
18

LOVER

Ford: Get home safe?

Lake: Yup. Thank you for showing me around your town and introducing me to your friends. They are all wonderful and I really enjoyed myself.

Ford: Don't thank me. You gave me the best week of my life, Red. If you take one thing from our week together, please let it be that. You're in charge. You call the shots. Demand what you want and take it. You've fucking earned it.

Lake: It was the best week of my life, too.

Lake: Thanks for the flowers. They're beautiful.

Ford: Amanda said the show was incredible. Keep kicking ass.

Lake: I got my hair cut today.

Ford: Yeah?

> Lake: I didn't have the nerve to chop it all off.
> \<pic of Lake smiling\>

> Ford: Gorgeous as always, Red. And you had the balls to do what you wanted. That's all I meant that night. You're in control.

> Lake: Doesn't feel like it. Feels like the only things I want are the things I can't have.

> Ford: You can have it all. Just have to ask for it.

> Lake: Have you spoken to your kids?

> Ford: Daniel and I are meeting at the rink tomorrow. No word from Millie or Paul.

I scroll through our messages while I wait for the show to start. Messages. That's all I have left of him. Even the marks he left on my body have all disappeared. I cried when I woke up to discover the last bruise had faded.

"Almost ready?" Amanda asks, her smile big.

To protect my vocal cords, I don't speak before shows, so I give her a nod and haul myself to my feet. It takes everything in me to pull my shoulders back and smile like I'm excited for tonight.

The crowd's energy is such a welcome blessing. It worms its way into me, breathing life into my lungs and into my soul. And despite my previously melancholy mood, I walk offstage at the end of the night feeling like I've gone through a full spectrum of emotions. Singing about heartbreak and love so soon after experiencing both is new for me. It's excruciating at times, but working through it all this week has made me a better musician. It's one more thing Ford gave me. It's not all bruises and messages after all. My career will be better for the time I spent with him.

So much for swearing no man can take credit for my career.

I toss my head back and laugh at myself as I make my way to my dressing room. It's the first time I've truly felt light in a week. God, I hope the sensation remains after tonight. Refusing to sulk for another minute, I decide I'll find Amanda and see if she wants to come with me to the nearest, loudest bar and grab a drink. I don't want to talk, but at least I won't be alone.

When I walk into my dressing room, though, my heart stops. She's here, but she's got company. Devastatingly handsome and yet a bit disheveled, Ford Hall standing in front of me takes my breath away. I blink twice to make sure I'm not hallucinating as a labyrinth of emotions fight to break free.

As soon as he spots me, the biggest smile I've ever seen from him splits his face. Then he's moving toward me, his gaze focused, his movements steady.

"I'll leave you two alone," Amanda says, disappearing from the room.

Two feet in front of me, Ford pauses and curls his hands into fists at his sides, like he can't keep them still. "You were incredible tonight."

"You were watching?" I whisper.

Dipping his chin, he gives me a subtle nod. "I—uh—brought ice cream." He holds out a hand, palm up, gesturing to the table in front of the small couch. Two crystal sundae bowls filled with chocolate ice cream, a mountain of whipped cream, and chocolate shavings sit side by side.

I blink at the display, baffled. What is he doing here? And why are there lit candles on either side of the sundaes? "Ice cream?"

"Frozen hot chocolate. You still haven't had it, right? Fuck." He roughs a hand over his chin. "Tell me I'm not too late."

"Too late?" I'm like a parrot, mimicking his every word. Sweat trickles down my neck as I gape at him. Without looking away, I lift my hair and fan myself. "Is it hot in here?"

The devastating smile I missed so much spreads across Ford's face, and his stormy eyes pool inky black as he holds his arm out in front of him. "Here, put your hair up."

My heart stutters at the sight of a fucking scrunchie on his wrist.

The hot pink elastic pops against his tan skin and white dress shirt. Is this man kidding me right now?

When I don't make a move to take it—I'm too busy melting into a puddle—he lets out a frustrated breath, circles me, and grasps the makeshift ponytail I'm holding on to. He brushes my hand away and ties the strands into a loose ponytail, cooling me instantly. Just as quickly, though, my body heats again. This time it's from his proximity. Ford presses his thick frame against my back and holds himself there, towering over me. Rather than dominating, his presence is comforting. He sucks in a deep breath, and then his lips brush against my neck in a featherlight touch. "Please have ice cream with me, Red."

I take in the setup, practically floating. "Why did you bring ice cream?"

"Because *Serendipity* is your favorite movie, and you deserve the treat."

I smile as I peer back at him over my shoulder. "It's from Serendipity?"

Ford nods. "Flew it here myself. I took it out of the freezer a few minutes ago. I would have waited if I realized you'd have so many questions. It's probably melting." He chuckles, though the sound is equal parts humor and uncertainty. He's nervous, and it's absolutely adorable on a man who is used to being so sure of himself in everything he does.

I slide my hand in his and step forward, leading him to the couch. Before I can sit, I notice the television on the opposite wall. It's on, and it's paused on the opening credits of my favorite movie.

"Dammit," I mutter, my eyes welling with tears. I have to release my hold on him to swipe away the evidence of my insanity.

Ford doesn't allow it, though. He snatches my hand before I can bat at the tears. Then he shuffles closer and presses his palms to either side of my neck, his thumbs holding me in place, eyes filled with concern as he dips closer. "What's wrong?"

I huff out a deep breath. "I can't even fling right."

His brows crease in confusion. "Huh?"

I roll my eyes, but it's not at this sweet man. He's been everything he promised he'd be. "I did it again. Fell for someone unavailable. God damnit," I growl, trying to step back. If I don't put some distance between myself and this perfect date that Ford set up, then I'll ask him to stay and put his babies inside me. What the hell is wrong with me? Why do I always fall for unavailable men?

Ford's lips tip up in the hint of a smile. "You falling for me, Red?"

I wave my hand and scoff, but it only makes him smile bigger.

"Obviously not," I mutter. "It's just, no one ever goes out of their way for me, and here you are, flying ice cream in from a place featured in my favorite movie." I narrow my eyes on him and poke him in the chest. "Who does that?"

The laugh he barks out is loud and free and filled with joy. "Let me get this straight. You're mad at me because I brought you ice cream? Because I did something thoughtful?"

"Fuming, actually." I back away and pace across the room. "You told me this was a fling. We agreed it would be over when I went back on tour. But then you go and do the swooniest fucking things. *Ford*," I say, the single word a plea, "this is husband level shit. You don't do stuff like this for flings." Hand on my hip, I stare him down. "You actually aren't very good at flinging either."

He eats up the space between us until we're practically touching. "I never said it was a fling."

"Yes you—" I snap my mouth shut and rack my brain for the memory. Didn't he use that term? *Fling*?

"No." He cups my cheeks, forcing me to hear his every word. "You told me to let go if I didn't want you to kiss me."

I nod as I'm taken back to that moment only two weeks ago. To New Year's Eve. The night everything was set in motion.

"I didn't let go then, and I sure as fuck am not letting go now."

My heart clenches so tightly I have to press a palm to my chest to ease the ache. "What are you saying?"

"If I thought we'd be nothing more than a fling, Lake, then I would have let go. I wouldn't have let us burn our reputations to the ground for something so small. I'd have given a fuck."

"So this isn't a fling?" I whisper, clutching at his shirt, holding on for dear life.

He caresses my cheeks with his thumbs and hovers closer. "No, baby, this isn't a fling."

Anticipation coils low in my belly, and a shy smile peeks through. "So you like me?"

Ford's relieved smile is devastating. "I'm fucking gone for you, Red."

Trembles overtake me as he presses his lips to mine. As our tongues tangle, he drinks up my moans like the most satisfying glass of whiskey, savoring each gasp and whimper.

"Fuck, I missed you."

There's no air left in my lungs. Dizzy and speechless, I claw at his thick hair, desperate for more. With a groan, he pulls back and smiles at me. "Ice cream, baby. My girl deserves her first date."

"We're really going to date?"

Grasping my hand, Ford leads me to the couch, then he pulls me onto his lap. "I'm going to date the fuck out of you."

I laugh as I push against his chest, but he holds me in place. Giving up the fight, I settle in and relax in his arms. I'm struck by the love I see in his eyes. Slate blue heated with a mix of affection and desire. God, he's beautiful.

"I'm in love with you, Lake Paige. With all of you. The girl who's always so goddamn polite, and the girl who takes what she wants. The musician, the naughty girl hidden behind that sugary façade. The sweetheart who loves big and feels too much. I can't think of a goddamn thing I don't love about you. And I can't fucking live without you."

Tears flood my eyes as I press my lips to his. "I love you too, Ford Hall."

His gruff laughter cuts our kiss short. "I take that back. There's one thing I can't fucking stand."

My mouth falls open in shock, but he smiles as he kisses me again. "Your last name. I hate that it's not mine. Seriously, Lake, if it wasn't insane, I'd get down on my knees right now and beg you to spend your life with me. Beg you to become Lake Hall."

There's power in knowing precisely what you want. But the true power comes when you ask for it.

"I like being insane with you. And I like you even more on your knees, Mr. Hall."

EPILOGUE

SWEET NOTHING

Settled on Ford's lap, I sip from his mug of coffee while he reads the paper. This is how we spend our mornings now that the tour has come to an end. While I finished out the last leg, Ford followed me from stop to stop, working remotely. He refused to leave me for even one night after he showed up with ice cream for our "first date."

Our new kitten, Sera, short for Serendipity, jumps up onto the table, and I scoop her into my lap while Ford lets out a gruff harrumph. I press a kiss to his cheek, earning myself a smile before he goes back to reading the paper. These are the moments I live for. When it's just me and the man I love hidden away in our house on the water in the most beautiful small town.

Buttons and my white cat Lyric are cuddled on the floor by our feet.

"Oh shit," Ford says, holding out the paper for me to see.

"Beckett Langfield Picks Pinup Models over Preschoolers," I read. The article goes on to explain how the owner of the Boston Revs turned down a charity event for kids in favor of the swimsuit models. "That's some bad press."

With a laugh, Ford pries Sera out of my arms and sets her on the floor, though he's sure to give her a good nuzzle before he shifts me so that I am straddling him and drags his hands up under the fabric of my shirt.

"I'm sure his head of PR will be busy trying to spin that."

I laugh as I press my palms to his chest. "Poor Liv." I've met Olivia Maxwell, the woman who handles PR for Langfield Corp on a few occasions. She certainly has her hands full with Gavin and Beckett and both sports teams.

Ford strokes a thumb over my nipple, and I arch into him. When I let loose a moan, power flares in his eyes. "You wet for me already, Red?"

His voice taunts me. It's dark and twisted how much I love when he treats me like this.

I roll my hips against his erection, and he lifts my shirt, taking my nipple between his teeth. The pain of the bite only spurs me to rock against him in a steady rhythm. In seconds, I'm ready to combust. He laves the nipple, soothing it for a moment before giving the same attention to the other.

"Yes," I chant, encouraging him. "Please, Ford."

"Please what, baby? What does my gorgeous girl need right now?" Lust-filled eyes drink me in as his hands smooth up and down my hips and thighs. His thumb skates beneath my cotton pajama shorts, pushing upward until he reaches my pubic bone. "That's my good girl. No panties. Are you soaking my cock right now? Gushing for me?"

His words flicker through my body like a lick of heat, and I fall back, giving him more access.

Ford chuckles darkly against my belly as he lifts me up and settles me on the kitchen table. He's got my shorts off a heartbeat later, and then his palms are pushing my thighs apart. From between my legs, he looks up at me, tortured and beautiful. "Always sparkling for me." He glides his tongue between my lips.

The move sends a shudder rippling through me, and I spiral in anticipation of the sweet release he's going to bring me. I close my eyes, enjoying the way his tongue works me over, and groan when he adds a finger and fucks me with both that and his tongue until I'm panting. But it's not enough. All I want is his cock. Need it really.

"Ford," I purr. "Please."

His breath tickles the tender skin of my inner thighs as he laughs. He knows exactly what I need. "You feeling empty, Red? Need me to fill you?"

"God, yes," I mutter.

The slap to my clit is so surprising I almost come on the spot.

"Ford," he reminds me, the single word rough. "It's only my name on that tongue when you're coming."

"Then hurry the fuck up and give me my cock already!"

He takes half a step back and drops his pants. Then he's fisting his shaft and torturing me as he rubs it against my swollen clit. "This cock? You demanding this one?" he teases, possessive pride in his expression. It's how he always is. Constantly fighting for me to fight for what I want. To fight for myself.

"Yes, Ford. I need it."

Hovering close, he kisses me, his cock heavy against my clit as he does. "Whatever my girl wants, she gets." Then he arches back and crosses my legs, making me impossibly tight as he slides inside me and thrusts slowly, drawing out the pleasure. "Play with your clit, baby. I want you to milk my cock."

We go on like that until we're both pulsing and cursing and panting our *I love yous* into the new day. After we've both come, he pulls out and hands me my shorts.

When the doorbell rings, a devilish smile takes over Ford's face. "Forgot to mention Paul was stopping by."

I race to put on my shorts as he heads for the door. Halfway there, he hollers, "And don't you even think about cleaning yourself up." He turns around, and his gaze captures me. "I want you dripping with me until I tell you to stop."

Oh my god. My pussy spasms in response to his words, sending the first drops of his pleasure leaking from me. I blink a few times and blow out a calming breath. Then I rush to the sink so I can wash my hands and quickly fix my hair before my ex appears.

We've yet to meet face to face since he blew up my entire life, and

I oddly don't feel much of anything about it. Other than sticky, since his father made a complete mess out of me.

I know when he's gone, Ford will force us both into the shower and probably make me come a couple more times. Then we'll spend the afternoon lazing around before heading to dinner with Nate and Amelia. Life in this small town is at complete odds with the life I was leading only a month ago, but I've settled in quickly. Most days I still can't believe how at home I feel here.

I'm tempted to say thank you to Paul. His actions forced me to step out of my comfort zone. Pushed me to search for what truly made me happy. When his father steps back into the room wearing a big smile and spins me so I can face my ex, I know without a doubt that things are exactly as they were meant to be.

Paul shakes his head, eyes wide as he looks from me to Ford and back again. "I can't believe this. My dad's actually your boyfriend?"

"No." I wiggle my fingers, letting the rock on my hand sparkle in the kitchen light. His dad is my fiancé. "But karma is."

THE END

EXTENDED EPILOGUE

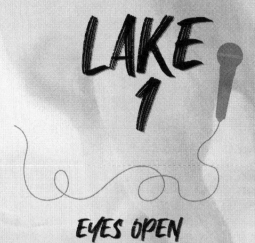

LAKE
1

EYES OPEN

A nd then they lived happily ever after.

Except the real work starts after those seven words.

Sure, my ex was hit with a heavy dose of karma when I fell in love with his father. And he'd earned it.

But karma has a way of making Thanksgiving dinners and Christmas gatherings uncomfortable. Karma kind of feels empty every time I watch my husband flounder for a way to repair his relationship with his child.

Also being a constant meme on TikTok has gotten old. The clips of me exiting a hotel with my ex's dad are still trending.

Surprisingly, it isn't Ford's relationship with Paul that has suffered since we went public. My ex didn't seem all that bothered, honestly.

It was his daughter Millie who has the hardest time.

There was a time when she liked me. I even would have considered us friends.

But now it's not just the media painting me as the brutal woman who took no prisoners as she sought revenge. It's my husband's flesh and blood.

Couple that with the restlessness that's plagued me and the discontent I feel when it comes to my career, and I've got a serious case of anxiety about this weekend.

"Red, you almost ready?" My husband hollers from downstairs.

Our engagement was short, and we were married in Aruba, in front of our closest friends and family. It was a magical week. One I hoped would give me time with Millie and allow me to show her that I'm not the vengeful person the media has made me out to be. That I'm just a girl who fell head over heels in love with her father.

But rather than stay the week as planned, Millie left the morning after the wedding and unexpectedly picked up and moved to Paris.

It hurts Ford, that she'd run so far, though she claims she left for a job opportunity she couldn't pass up. But when I bring it up, he says it will just take her time.

Apparently time is up, though.

Today, we're headed to Vegas to watch Daniel, Ford's third child, play hockey, and Millie is coming with us. I have a show this weekend too, so my time will be split and hopefully that will allow Ford some quality time with his daughter.

I stare down at my phone screen, at the app I just downloaded, conflicted. Worried about how Ford will react yet giddy at the idea of it.

"Coming," I reply as I close out of the app and pocket my phone with a shaky hand. Then I grab my carry on and bound down the stairs.

"You aren't yet but you will be soon," Ford says in that way that sends an arc of electricity straight to my core. He's standing at the bottom of the steps with a smile on his face.

God my husband is sexy as fuck. His dark hair is sprinkled with a bit more pepper than it was when we fell in love last year. As much as I love the contrast, it's a reminder of the stress he tries to hide from me.

He scans me from head to toe, his blue eyes bright and a wicked smile growing as he holds out his arms to pull me close. "Fuck Red, should I tell them to take their own plane?"

I nuzzle into his chest, both dreading this trip and knowing it's time to stop avoiding my fears.

At the sound of his phone, Ford slips one hand into his pocket and pulls his phone out. He slides his finger across the screen, then taps the speaker icon. "Hey Gav, ready for Vegas?"

My husband's best friend's voice booms through the speaker. "Was wondering if you had room on that jet of yours for another traveler?"

Ford shifts, though he doesn't let go of me, as he takes Gavin off speaker and brings the phone to his ear. "What's going on?"

Nerves course through me, bringing with them a wave of unease. I have a feeling I know what's going on but I don't want to be right. A few months ago, the night of Daniel's graduation party, I got up to go to the bathroom in the middle of the night. On my way back to bed, I heard a noise, so I peeked out the balcony door. Even now, I'm not exactly sure what I saw. It was dark and the hot tub is at least thirty feet from our bedroom but there were definitely two people in the water, and from the way the woman was bouncing, it's hard to deny what they were doing.

I couldn't see her face since her back was to me, but the only female still here when I went to bed was Millie and the man in the hot tub was one thousand percent Gavin.

"Yeah, of course you can fly with us. Mills is coming too, did I tell you that?" My oblivious husband drawls.

Well, this trip just got a hell of a lot more interesting.

FORD
2

THE ARCHER

"Holy shit this is sick," Gavin says as he steps onto my wife's plane.

I laugh as I stand up to greet him. "My girl does well," I say with a wink at Lake.

Cheeks pink, she shakes her head.

"I've gotta take a video of this for Beckett, he's gonna be pissed when he finds out it's so much nicer than ours," Gavin says as he yanks his phone from his pocket. Seconds later, he's taking pictures, then recording what can only be described as an "MTV Cribs style" tour of the plane. He drops a kiss on Lake's cheek as he passes her.

He doesn't notice how distracted she is, but I do.

Before we got together, Lake was always friendly, always polite. It's what used to drive me nuts about her. She's still one of the kindest people I know, and I love it, but she's grown a backbone in the last year or so. Now, though, I worry that she's fallen back into her old ways. She's hiding something. She's…Fuck, is she unhappy?

Our life has been moving at warp speed since last year. First she had to finish her tour, then we immediately jumped into wedding planning. We took a little time off for a long honeymoon, but the moment we returned to the real world, she joined me in the office as co-owner of my record label. When she isn't writing her own music or preparing for her next album release, she's helping up and coming artists find their path in this business.

She's got to be exhausted.

But is she unhappy?

With Gavin busy zooming in on every detail, I check in with her. "C'mere Red."

Lake's blue eyes find mine and her face lights up, calming me almost instantly. This fucking woman of mine is gorgeous, but more than that, she's the most genuine person I've ever met.

"You excited for the weekend?" she asks as she settles against my chest. We're waiting for Millie's flight from Paris to arrive before we take off.

"Excited to spend time with you." I press a kiss to her forehead and brush her cheek with my thumb. "And to see Daniel play and spend time with Mills."

It's been forever since my whole family was in the same place. Even Paul plans to fly out for the game.

Things are better with him. I wouldn't say he and Lake will be spending time together but they get along for my sake.

Is that what's bothering her? That we'll be seeing Paul?

"Daddy!"

My focus is pulled from Lake at the sound of Millie's voice.

"Millie Rosemarie Hall," I say, my whole being lighter now that she's here. "Look at how beautiful you are!"

Lake lets go of me, and I launch to my feet and scoop my daughter up into a hug.

"Please, I look like a dead rat after that long flight but you are a sight for sore eyes." She squeezes me tight in return.

"Hey Millie," Gavin says from behind me, apparently having finished his tour.

My daughter steps back and gives my friend a shy wave. "Hey Gavin, good to see you." Then she turns to Lake and to my surprise wraps her in a hug. "Hi Lake."

She lets go of her quickly but my grin is wide either way. She's coming around.

"Alright get comfortable," I tell my crew. "I'll go let the pilot know we're ready to head out."

When I come back my wife is seated across from Gavin and Millie. My gut twists as I take Lake in. She's curled in on herself, looking down at her phone. The antisocial behavior is so unlike her.

Gavin is talking to Millie, his voice low, but as I step up beside them, he goes quiet and looks up at me. "We all set?"

I glance at Lake again, then nod at Gavin. "Yeah. We'll be up in five. Big plans tonight?"

Gavin shakes his head. "Nah, I rarely go out anymore."

"Why are you flying out before the team then?" Lake asks, a line forming between her brows.

Gavin leans back in his seat and grasps the armrests. "There's a great center playing at a high school right off the strip. I'm going to stop by and watch him practice since their game this weekend is at the same time as ours."

Gavin's the general manager of the Boston Bolts. If not for my full schedule I'd love to join him. See how his brain works when he scouts future members of my son's team.

"That's so cool," Millie says.

I laugh at what almost sounds like genuine interest in her tone. "I don't remember you ever once wanting to attend one of your brothers practices in high school."

My daughter's cheeks turn rosy. "Whatever Dad, I'm just trying to make conversation with your friend."

Chuckling, I turn to Lake, expecting to find her laughing too. Instead, she's staring at her damn phone again. When she feels my eyes on her she immediately flips it over so that I can't see the screen.

My stomach bottoms out. Something is going on with my wife and I'm going to get to the bottom of it.

LAKE

DON'T BLAME ME

Mel: Did you tell Daddy yet?

Me: LOL he would die if he read that.

Mel: Oh excuse me, must use his proper name. Did you tell Daddy Ford yet?

Me: Ugh, no. I'm so nervous.

Mel: Why? You know that man adores you. Just tell him the truth.

I chew on my lip, tracking Ford as he walks out of the bathroom dressed in a black suit. Damn, he is the most beautiful thing I've ever seen. Before he reaches me, I flip my phone over so he doesn't see the text messages.

I will tell him. Just not this weekend. There's too much going on between rehearsals, my show, and Daniel's game. Not to mention he really should focus on his other kids, especially Millie, while we're here. I get him to myself so often, and it would be selfish of me to steal even an extra second of his time.

"You feeling okay, baby?" Ford stops in front of me, scrutinizing me with a frown.

Skin heating beneath his gaze, I fan myself. "Fine. Just probably a little jet lag."

He reaches out to help me up. "We'll get you a cup of tea on the way down to rehearsal. Don't push too hard tonight. You could do this set in your sleep."

I force a smile. I definitely could. That's part of what's bothering me. I don't want to do this set anymore. I don't want to do a lot of the things I've done in the past. Somewhere along the line, my outlook has changed, and dancing around on stage no longer feels right for me.

I'm far more comfortable sitting in our living room, guitar on my lap, the fire roaring in the hearth, and my husband in a chair watching me from behind the lenses of those black-framed glasses of his.

"You should go to dinner with Millie, no need for you to come to my rehearsal."

He snags his glasses from the nightstand and slips them into his coat pocket. Then he grabs my phone which is still on the bed and slides it into his pocket. "You're always leaving this behind."

I shrug. "I don't have anywhere to put it in my outfit for the show."

Ford's eyes heat. Though I may be over the shows, Ford very clearly still loves the costumes. "No you definitely don't." Pressing closer, he settles his hands on my ass cheeks and squeezes. "And if you think I'm leaving you in a room full of people while you're wearing this silky getup, you've lost your goddamn mind, Red."

I roll my eyes. "You're a caveman."

"And you love it." He presses his lips to mine and every worry and concern slips through the cracks. This man always eases my burdens, even when he doesn't realize it. He's the best damn thing that has ever happened to me.

"Fuck," he rasps, grinding his cock against me. "If I don't get you to practice asap, I'm going to fuck you right here."

I slide my tongue across his lips. "Promise?"

"Wife, the things I'm going to do to your body tonight..."

My thighs clench at the visions of what he might come up with. "Remember the first time we were in a hotel?"

Head lowered, he presses warm open mouthed kisses against my neck. "How could I forget? Had these delicious tits pressed against the glass while I fucked you from behind."

The walls of my pussy spasm. "Oh shit," I murmur. "We're going to be late."

"Are you dripping for me, wife? If I slide my hand between your thighs right now, what would I find?"

I buck against him, searching for friction. "Please," I whisper.

"Please what?"

"Fuck me."

"With what?" This question is a deep rumble that vibrates through me.

Delirious with lust, I shake my head. "Your fingers, your tongue, your cock, I don't care just *fuck* me."

Ford's chuckle is dark, sinister, as he licks a path between my breasts. "You'd like that wouldn't you? You'd like to walk into rehearsal with my cum seeping down your leg. Marked by me."

It's dirty the image he paints and it only leaves me wetter, panting for him. "Yes. Do that."

He sinks his teeth into the top of my breast, and my body jolts with pure need.

For the first time in I don't know how long I'm not focused on being the perfect musician, perfect business partner, perfect step-mother. All I want to be is the reckless slut that Ford uses for his plea-sure. I want the two of us to be people who care about nothing but one another and our pleasure. As desire winds through me, I no longer care how late I am for rehearsal.

"On your knees," I hiss.

In his dark suit, my husband drops to the floor without hesitation.

The pleased expression he wears, the joy that comes with satisfying me reflected in his blue irises, leaves me ripe with power.

"Now what?" he grits out.

That power makes me so dizzy, I have to rest a hand on his shoulder for balance. "Slide my panties down."

Smiling wickedly, he obeys, tugging the fabric down and supporting me as I step out. Then he lifts the panties to his nose, inhaling. "Fucking perfection, Red." He slides them into his pocket then stares up at me. "Am I down here for a reason?"

With my lip caught between my teeth, I lift one black heel and settle it on his shoulder.

He hisses as he wraps his fingers around my ankle.

"Hurt?" I ask.

Kissing the inside of the joint, he shakes his head. "No, Red. But if you don't tell me to put my tongue on your pussy I may die."

I drop my head back and laugh. "Fine, you've been a good boy so far, have at it."

Ford pushes me back toward the edge of the bed and adjusts my legs so they're both on his shoulders, then he grins and whispers "Thank you beautiful," before sliding his tongue between my lips.

Each swipe feels like magic, allowing my body to slowly let go of the stress I've been holding on to. He paints pleasure over my body and it's not long before I'm panting heavily and close to coming.

"Are you hard husband? Are you dripping for me?"

He chuckles against my pussy, then kisses my clit and looks up from his position on the floor. "What do you think, Red? I've got your taste on my tongue, your scent surrounding me and your fucking red lips telling me how good I make you feel." He slides a finger inside me and rolls a circle around my clit with his thumb. "I'm fucking ready to hump the floor for a little relief. Of course I'm leaking. The question is are you going to let me come down your throat or am I going to fill up this cunt."

I want him to tie me up. I want him to use me for hours. But we don't have hours. "Pinch my clit and make me come. Then you can fuck me from behind and pull my hair."

"Everyone will know you've been a dirty little slut, Red." He does as I've commanded, pinching my clit between two fingers. The act is harsh enough to make me scream. As I arch in pained pleasure, he puts his hot mouth on me and sucks on the sensitive bead, all while he works his fingers in and out of me, sending me hurtling toward a release so violent I buck off the bed. With a hand on his head, I grip his hair and pull, keeping him in place, encouraging him to lap at me through my orgasm. I've barely taken a breath before he's flipping me over and slamming into me, already groaning and swelling even thicker. With one arm banded around me, he works my clit again as he thrusts into me riotously. "Everyone will know your husband fucked you good. That you couldn't wait for this cock. Right Red. You had to have it." As his body goes rigid and he comes, pulsing deep within me, I shatter beneath him.

"Yes. I needed it," I cry. "Need you." Tears stream down my face. I need him so much and I'm so scared to tell him everything. So scared to lose this.

He must hear it in my voice, in my moans, because he pulls out and quickly draws me to him, then sinks back inside me still half hard. "Baby, please, what's going on?" he whispers. He doesn't pull out. He doesn't thrust. He just holds me.

I shake my head and bury my face in his neck. "Later. Right now just hold me, Ford. Tell me you love me, tell me you'll always love me, no matter what."

He threads his fingers through my hair and tugs, forcing me to look up into his beautiful blue eyes. "Forever, Red. No matter what. You're my entire world. I love you."

I nod, seeing the truth of his words. "I love you, too."

FORD
4

SAY DON'T GO

As my wife fixes herself in the bathroom mirror, I watch her closely, still so fucking uneasy.

"Promise I won't disappear if you look away," she teases softly.

I squeeze my fists, heart aching. "You don't look away from perfection," I rasp.

Her shoulders tighten and her eyes flutter shut. "I'm not perfect."

With my hands on her shoulders, I press a kiss to her neck and meet her eye in the mirror. "To me you are. *For me* you are."

My phone buzzes, and at the sound, Lake slips out of my hold.

"Could be Millie," she says. "You should check it. And I should head to rehearsal." She steps into me again and presses a kiss to my lips. Before I can reciprocate, she disappears, leaving me in the brightly lit bathroom alone.

Distracted, I answer the phone without bothering to look at who's calling. "Hello."

"Hey, up for a drink?" Gavin asks.

I sigh and he laughs.

"Jeez," he huffs. "Don't sound so excited."

"Sorry, it's just—" I swipe a hand over my face and shuffle back into the bedroom. "Something is going on with Lake."

"Shit, you okay?"

"Yeah." I sigh as the ball of dread in my gut grows. "I'll meet you for a drink at the bar near the lobby. Do you mind if I ask Millie to join? She might still be sleeping but if not I'll see if she wants dinner too. Lake is going to be at rehearsal for a while."

"Yeah, sure. And listen, if you feel like you need to leave so you can be with Lake, I can entertain Millie for a bit."

I smile. "You're a good friend, Gavin. Appreciate you. I'll see you downstairs."

THE CASINO IS loud and full of flashing lights from the machines. As I weave through all the people spending money they likely don't have, I spot Millie and Gavin standing at the bar. Gavin's grinning, clearly being funny, as he always is, and Millie grasps his arm, leaning into him.

My stomach clenches at the moment I've just witnessed. What the–

My phone buzzes in my pocket, distracting me. Fuck, I hope it's Lake.

> Mel: I know you're worried about how Ford will react but you've got this. I love you and I'm here for you. You're the best damn person I know and if he doesn't want this then fuck him.

> Mel: But also, he totally loves you and it's all going to be FINE.

I BLINK and reread the messages. Only when I've read them for a third time do I realize the phone I'm holding isn't mine. It's Lake's. Fuck.

It takes me seconds to decide that I'm going to violate my wife's privacy, and with a sharp breath in, I open the text message thread and scroll up so I can read the messages that started earlier this evening.

Mel: Did you tell Daddy yet?

Lake: LOL he would die if he read that.

Mel: Oh excuse me, must use his proper name. Did you tell Daddy Ford yet?

Lake: Ugh, no. I'm so nervous.

MY STOMACH SINKS. What is my wife nervous about? How could I have failed her so badly? Because I clearly have if she thinks she has anything to be worried about when it comes to me.

I reread the thread three more times before I hear Gavin calling my name.

"You gonna join us?" he asks, wearing his signature smile.

Thank fuck, there seems to be a bit more distance between him and my daughter.

I shake my head, pretty positive I imagined an intimacy that doesn't exist. Clearly, I've got more important things to worry about than my best friend going anywhere near my 23 year old daughter. He would never.

I stride up to them and kiss Millie on the cheek. "Hey baby girl."

"Hi daddy, you okay?"

I sigh, feeling like an ass for doing this. I've barely spent time with my daughter since my wedding since she's living in Paris and working for Gavin's sister. But if I stay, I'll be shit company. There's no way I can concentrate on anything until I find out what is going on with my wife.

I hold up Lake's phone as if that's the issue. "Lake left her phone in the room. I gotta go drop this off at rehearsal. Will you guys be okay without me for a bit?"

"Of course Daddy, I'm probably going to head to bed shortly anyway," Millie says around a yawn. "We can do dinner tomorrow night after Daniel's game though, right? Before Lake's show?"

I pull her close and hug her tight. "Yes. And breakfast tomorrow morning with both your brothers. Okay?"

My beautiful girl smiles. "You got it."

Turning to my friend, I hold a hand out. "Sorry about this."

"Not a problem," Gavin says easily, slipping his hand into mine and shaking it. "Mills and I will finish these drinks and then I'll probably grab room service."

I glance at them both again, trying to force my mind to let go of the awful things I just accused my best friend of in my head. I've got to get a handle on whatever is going on with Lake before I go and destroy every other relationship I have by lashing out unnecessarily.

FORD
5

SO IT GOES

As my wife rehearses one song, then another, it's clear that she's off. I'm restless. I want to jump in. But this is her job—it's mine too—I have to control myself. But when her damn phone beeps again, there's no fighting the urge to check the notification.

When the alert on the screen registers, my heart drops.

You're ovulating!

She's what?

I glance from the device to the stage where my wife is currently running through another dance move, then back again.

She's ovulating…She's ovulating. Holy fuck. My heart picks up, and blood whooshes in my ears. My wife wants to have a baby.

I zero in on her again and my lips pull up. Lake wants to have my baby.

The primal wave that flows through me can't be described as anything but pure animalistic lust. As I watch the woman I love with all of my goddamn heart and knowing she wants to start a family with me, it all falls into place.

Her stress. The tears. The worry.

The text messages.

She's afraid to tell me she wants to have a baby. Nervous that I won't want it too.

Which is absurd. Though I suppose, with our age difference, it's understandable. But I've done this dance. I love being a parent. Though it's something I haven't experienced with her. And somehow I know this dance with her will be the sweetest one yet. Because the idea of Lake growing our child, the idea of seeing her swollen belly, of running to the store late at night to satisfy her pregnancy cravings, of spoiling her and loving on her and then watching her become a mother? Fuck. My heart beats so wildly it feels like it'll launch itself right out of my chest and cling to her.

I fucking love this woman and the life I'm conjuring. It would be a fucking dream to raise a child or two with her. The thoughts overtake me as my instincts take over and my feet move in her direction.

On stage she sings about our life in Bristol, how happy she is in the simplicity of it all.

I grin knowing this is only the beginning. "Everyone get the fuck out," I shout, my smile so big I probably look delirious.

Lake's eyes go wide, and she blinks at me. I catalog the way she flinches as she assesses me and silently works through her guilt. I'm unhinged, deranged, and she sees it. But she has to see my smile. She has to realize that I've never once raised my voice at her.

And that I'm always a complete professional.

Except when it involves her.

This woman makes me irrational. She tempts me to do things like record her as I fuck her in my office or push her against the glass of a high-rise hotel to fuck her for all the world to see.

The possessiveness and the need to prove she's mine over and over again, aren't signs of a grounded man and I couldn't give a fuck.

But now?

Now I need to have her. I need to fill her. She wants my baby? She wants me to impregnate her? I'm going to have her so full of me she'll walk out of here dripping.

I barely register as the crew on stage filters off.

Several of our employees side eye me but I pay them no attention.

No one dares to defy my request. This isn't how I normally act. Do they think I'm pissed? The smile probably betrays that notion.

I try to tamp down on the expression, hoping like hell they can't tell that what I actually want is the privacy to fuck my wife in public, right here on this stage.

It's poetic, if I'm being honest.

The first time I saw this woman she was on a stage. My perfect, put together wife. The woman coveted by the world. There isn't a man in his right mind who wouldn't want to switch places with me. There isn't a woman who wouldn't do anything for the chance to be her best friend.

But she's mine.

And soon she'll be the mother of my child.

Filled with purpose and hope and desire, I stalk toward the stage. I don't bother with the stairs. Instead, I launch myself up over the edge so that I'm standing before her.

"What are you–"

"You're ovulating." I keep my tone even, even as my insides are a riot of excitement.

Lake scrunches her nose adorably. "I'm what?"

Laughing, I pull her close. "Ovulating, Lake. You're ovulating right now. According to your app, at least." Holding up her phone, I show her the alert.

"Oh," she practically squeaks, grabbing for the device.

I tighten my grip and shove it back into my pocket, then settle my arms around her waist, holding her in place.

With an arched brow I regard her. "That all you have to say?"

She bites on her lip. "Um."

"Lake Hall, is there a reason you're acting confused right now? Demure? Quiet? What did I tell you when I asked you to marry me?"

She licks her red lips as she blinks up at me. "That you love me."

I chuckle. "I more than love you. You're my obsession, Red. I told you that you only have to tell me what you want and I'll give it to you. There is no ask too big. No request I'd deny."

A smile overtakes her, making that single dimple pop. "Ford."

"Lake," I chide. "What is it you want from me? Is it a baby? Is it a family? Because the idea of you wanting to have my child, the idea of filling you up over and over until you're pregnant with my baby? That is a dream fucking come true."

"It is?"

Squeezing her hips, I let out a dark chuckle. "You're going to pay for not talking to me first. For making me find out this way," I promise her. "But right now I need to fuck you."

She bites her lip. My girl does like her punishments. "Yeah?"

"Yeah," I grit out, tingles coursing down my spine in anticipation. "And for once the focus is going to be on my orgasm. Because that's what you need, don't you?"

She swipes her tongue across her lips.

"Words Red. Give Daddy your words."

That's it. With those words, her pupils blow wide. I've given her a smack when she used that name for me, but she's got a kink for it. And until this moment, I had no fucking idea I liked the sound of it. Maybe its because she was hiding from me. I clearly wasn't giving her what she needed. She needs more than just a man who worships her, who takes care of her.

And I'm going to give it all to her.

"I need your cum. Need you to fill me up."

I ghost my finger over her nipple which is hard beneath the silk top she's wearing.

"Daddy," she pants, her eyes fluttering shut.

Leaning in close, I brush my lips against her ear. "You're a dream come true, Lake." I press a kiss to her neck, and she exhales all of her stress. I bite down on her shoulder. "Hide from me again and I'll withhold orgasms for a week." I lick at the sting and pull the strap of her top off her shoulder, peppering kisses down her clavicle and onto her breast before swirling my tongue around her puckered nipple. With my free hand splayed across her back, I pull her closer so she can't escape the pain as I bite down. Then with her nipple in my mouth I look up, take her in.

She's magnificent. Her red lips swollen and falling open as she cries out.

"You're lucky your pussy is my favorite thing to eat. The taste of your pleasure dripping on my tongue is a craving I can't deny myself." I sink to my knees and take her pants with me.

A red silk thong covers her pussy but the evidence of her arousal stains it. She clearly changed after our earlier encounter because her other panties are still in my pocket.

I lean back on my haunches. "Get up on that pedestal and strip for me."

Lake shudders out a heady breath, but as if she can hear the impatience in my tone, she goes right for the three black stands rising from the stage. The two lower stands are where her dancers perform during the show. The center one, where she performs, is topped with a throne. She dances on and around it during one of her numbers.

"Highest one," I remind her.

That's where she belongs. In the center of a stage.

With a fist to my mouth, I watch as my gorgeous wife struts toward her throne. When she reaches the top, she stares at me and slowly fists the bottom of her silk top, then pulls it over her head.

Once it's fluttered onto the pedestal, she slips her thumbs inside the waistband of her panties and slides them down. When they hit her feet she steps out of one and then with a flick of her foot she kicks the damp fabric in my direction. As they land a few feet away, I crawl to grab them and pull them to my nose, inhaling my wife's excitement.

"That will earn you one orgasm," I tell her.

Lake's lips split into a beautiful smile. She does love to come.

"I really liked watching you crawl for my panties," she says in that husky voice that made her famous.

"You want me to crawl for you baby? I'd walk through fire for you, crawling is easy." I prowl toward her, my gaze locked with hers. Pleasure sweeps across her face as I get closer. I have no doubt she's gushing for me right now.

I climb onto the pedestal before her. "Sit on your throne, Red."

Obediently, she drops into the seat and crosses one leg over the other, bouncing her foot in anticipation.

"Spread those thighs, daddy needs room to work."

A flush creeps up her chest and neck as she grips the golden arms on the chair and swings her legs open, giving me the most gorgeous view.

Swollen lips, glistening pink, and begging for my tongue.

From my position on the pedestal beside her, I'm in the perfect position for what I want to do. I grip the throne and pull her closer, then then lean in, inhaling her. "I don't think I'll ever get enough of this. Of you like this. My perfect whore of a wife begging for my tongue." I flick her clit. Back and forth. Left and right. "No one gets to see you like this but me. They think you're America's sweetheart, but we both know better." I suck her clit into my mouth, maintaining eye contact, and she lets out the most beautiful sound. More beautiful than anything she's ever sung. Her moans are a symphony I'll never tire of. No music could ever compare to the sound my wife makes when I please her. As the theater goes quiet, I realize what I need.

"Your mic is on your shirt?"

Sucking in a breath, she nods. I snatch the silk top from the pedestal and push it toward her. "Turn it on."

Lake smirks, her eyes wide and full of desire. "What are you thinking?"

"I'm thinking I want to fill this entire theater with your moans. I'm thinking that I want to experience your slutty mouth begging for my cum in surround sound."

Lake's hands shake as she struggles to get the mic on. She's so worked up.

"Test it," I tell her when it's in place.

"Testing one—" Her voice booms around us.

"Red," I warn. She knows what I want her to test out. Not that fucking nonsense.

She giggles. "Please daddy, make me come," she pants, leaning into the sultry tone she's so good at.

"Hope you enjoyed being a wise ass, Red. How about you sing

your first number, and we see how long you last before you come apart at the seams."

Her eyes bulge, and her breath catches.

"Come on Red, I am the head of your label." I glower at her. "Perform for me."

Determination has her arching forward and becoming the performer she is on stage.

I chuckle. I'll have her turning into my whore of a wife in point two seconds. It's fun, this game we play.

But it is a game. We both know I worship her. That she's the light in my life. The beautiful sunset I crave daily.

The theater fills with the sound of her voice, pure and sweet. She's singing the song she wrote for us. A song about the beauty found in the quiet moments. When it's just us. Her in my lap, a newspaper in my hand. Our small town. Walks on the beach. Snowflakes on her cheeks.

I suck her clit into my mouth, and the words blur together, becoming a moan. I bite down on it, and she digs her fingers into my hair and pulls as she lets out a whine.

Plunging two fingers into her, I lap at her sopping pussy, and she grunts out a curse.

The music is lost and the room is filled with the sounds of her arousal. She pulses around my fingers, squeezing me tight.

"Please, please," she begs, her voice echoing, along with the wet sounds we make as I fuck her like this.

The sensation of my cock weeping for her flips a switch in my brain. Not a bead of precum should be wasted. The need to fill her is uncontrollable.

When I pull back, she whines, but a moment later, when I unbuckle my pants, that sound turns into a moan.

"You're too perfect like this, red. I'm dripping, but that cum is all for you. Beg for it, baby. Tell me you want Daddy to fill you up. That you want my cum. That you want my baby."

She nods, her eyes glazing over in excitement as she takes in my hard cock.

I stroke myself and lean in close, aligning my crown with her throbbing pussy. "You're going to squeeze it so tight, aren't you baby? You want every drop."

"Please Ford, please don't make me wait."

I smack her clit with the head of my cock. "What did you call me?"

"Daddy—" The word becomes a moan as I slam into her.

My lips find hers and our tongues tangle as I fuck her hard. I inhale her. Inhale this moment. We're making a baby. Suddenly, images of a life I've never pictured flit through me. Lake's swollen belly. Her holding an infant. The two of us watching our child take its first steps. Our kiss becomes more desperate. Fuck, it's like we're under a spell. Like she's seeing everything I'm seeing. Experiencing this moment as viscerally as I am.

"I love you," she whispers against my lips as her pussy quivers around me, milking my orgasm from my body. "Please fill me. Give me everything."

I come on a roar, my cock pulsing as I give her every ounce of my seed. With my arms wrapped around her, I lift her up and turn so that I'm sitting and she straddles my lap, still filled with me.

Hearts beating wildly, breaths ragged, we come down from the high. I rub her back slowly, unable to stop myself from touching her. The feel of her skin somehow grounds me to the moment.

"We're going to do that every day until you're pregnant with my baby," I tell her, one arm around her neck so that I can push her hair out of her face and kiss her.

Against my lips, Lake whispers the next words, changing my whole world. "You're going to be the best daddy, baby. I'm already pregnant."

LAKE
6

LABYRINTH

"You're pregnant?" Ford studies me, so very confused. "Baby, I know you're ovulating but there's a good chance it won't happen the first time."

My emotions are on overdrive. That was literally one of the hottest sexual experiences of my life, and that's saying something. My body is buzzing and my heart is still pounding uncontrollably. But I want this moment to be just for us so I search for the mic that Ford asked me to use and shut it off. Then I press my palms to his chest and ease back a fraction. "I'm pregnant. I took a test this morning. That's what I was worried about telling you. Not that I wanted to have a baby," I smile because I can't help it, "But that we are having a baby."

He blinks like he can't fathom it. "But the app said you were ovulating?"

"I downloaded it this morning so I could figure out how far along I am. I hadn't even input my last period when you interrupted me. It must have chosen a date by default."

Ford palms my face, both hands cradling my cheeks. "You're having my baby?" The words are filled with such wonder. Such love.

Tears breach my lids even as I try to blink them back. "Yes," I whisper.

"Holy fuck, you're really having my baby?" A smile blooms across his face and then he's kissing my lips and my tearstained cheeks. "I love you so much. This is the best fucking news."

"Really?"

Even though he's clearly happy, I can't silence the fears that snuck in earlier. That he'd feel trapped. Or disappointed that he had to go through all the stages of parenthood again.

Ford swipes a thumb against my falling tears and rubs his nose against mine. "My kids are the greatest accomplishments. They're my legacy. Kyla and I didn't always get it right but god I loved every moment of every stage. But Kyla wasn't the love of my life. And getting to do this with you?" He shakes his head like he's wonderstruck. "This is a gift, baby. Because while I will love all of our children equally, I have a feeling that experiencing parenthood with you will make these years the sweetest of my life."

There's no stopping the tears now that it's hit me: We're going to be parents. We're having a baby. And now that I'm not stressing about how he'll react to that news, now that I'm sitting with it, absorbing the implications, while we're still one like this, the emotions become too much. Through sobs I tell him the other things weighing on me. "I'd like tomorrow's show to be my last for a while. These next few years, this chapter we're entering, I want it to be just for us. I want to take our son or daughter to the park, not into stadiums. I want to gain weight and not stress about how I'll look for a concert. I want to wake up in your arms and know that my only job that day is to love you and our child."

Ford presses his lips to mine. "Done."

I suck in a breath. "That's it? You don't have anything else to say?"

My husband pulls me closer and kisses my forehead, then smooths a hand over my back, calming me. "I told you that I want to know your wants, your wishes. I want you to give me your commands. There isn't a thing I won't give you. You are the center of my world and now the mother of my child. You've given me a life I never could have dreamed of. I'm indebted to you for eternity, my love."

As I pull back so I can look at him, a sob escapes me. "You've given that all to me too. Two years ago I didn't think this life was possible. Everyone had a piece of me except me." I press my lips to his. "You helped me see that having all the things the world tells us are important means a whole lot of nothing if you're standing in a crowd, feeling completely alone. You are my souls counterpart and I can't wait to see you as a father to our child."

I'm shaking now as the air conditioning seeps into my sweaty skin. The instant I break out in goose bumps, Ford stands and carries me to where our clothes are strewn on the stage.

"Come on baby, we're going to get dressed and then we're going to get you a cup of tea and something to eat."

Once we're dressed, Ford wraps me in his suit jacket and lifts me into his arms, then heads for the exit.

"What are you doing?" I say with a squeal. "People are going to stare."

In response, he tightens his hold on me. "Had I known you were pregnant," he whispers, "I wouldn't have been so rough in there. Get used to being carried around, Red. For the next nine months your feet will barely touch the ground."

"I'm pregnant, I'm perfectly capable of walking," I complain, even though I'm wearing a smile. As we round the corner toward the restaurant, I spot Gavin and Millie walking out of it. "Oh—"

As Gavin threads his fingers with Millie's, I snap my mouth shut. Then, when he pushes her against the wall and whispers in her ear, I fight back a gasp.

Ford is focused on me, waiting for me to finish my sentence. When I don't he begins to turn in the direction I'm fixated on. Shoot. This is not good.

"Ahhh!" I scream, praying I can distract him before he sees them.

Ford's hold on me tightens. "What's wrong baby?"

"I just remembered that I want to have room service."

Ford frowns. "You screamed because you want room service?"

"No I screamed when I remembered how good the desserts are here. The baby is already craving sweets."

Ford chuckles and his hold on me relaxes. "Does the baby want an ice cream sundae?"

I tighten my hold on his neck and kiss him, hoping that Gavin and Millie will have moved on before I break our connection. Surely I screamed loud enough to get their attention, but I know all too well how oblivious people in love can be.

One day that is going to be a problem, but not today.

Tonight I'm stealing a few more simple moments with my husband.

SNEAK PEEK OF TROUBLE

Worst Human Alive: You really can't do anything right, can you? The first track was due to the label last week. Now you've up and disappeared for the holidays? What the hell are you thinking?

Worst Human Alive: You can't really believe you can hide from me.

Worst Human Alive: You're breaking your mother's heart. It's CHRISTMAS.

Worst Human Alive: Please, baby. I'm sorry. I promise things will be different. But you need to tell me where you are. Come home. We can fix this.

I stare at the new round of texts in an almost steady stream that hasn't stopped over the last two weeks. They've been coming in at regular intervals since I ran out of my apartment, leaving behind everything I owned, foolishly believing that I could just break up with him, and this would all end.

Worst Human Alive: I'm your fucking agent.
I'm legally entitled to know where you are.

A scoff full of rage bursts from me. The heat in my lungs makes me want to roar at the insanity of this situation.

He is my agent. He's also the person I loved for nearly a decade. My brother's best friend. The man my mother considers a second son. And my abuser.

God, why did it take me so long to figure out who he really was?

The tougher question is: If he hadn't done what he did the last time I saw him, would I have ever left? I don't want to even think about my answer. It'll only show how truly weak I am.

Melina Rodriguez: International Pop star. Three-time Grammy winner. Coward.

I power my phone off so that I don't have to be taunted by his constant musings tonight. Should I block him? Probably. But that will only make him more desperate. More dangerous. He's already more unhinged now that he doesn't know where I am.

I shake my head. "I shouldn't be here." Pushing my chair back from the counter, I clasp my hands in front of me and prepare to tell my best friend that I'm going to find a hotel in a city where no one will find me and lie low there.

"Of course you should be," Lake replies with a flip of her hand. As if she can magically change my mind.

Normally, she could. Lake gets her way with just about everyone. To the rest of the world, she's Lake Paige, the greatest female musician of our time. People are too enamored with my beautiful bestie to tell her no.

But to me, she's the girl who stayed up late after our shifts at the Bluebird to write music together. Who dreamed about sold-out bar shows while we ate ice cream on our worn brown couch in our tiny apartment in Nashville. The woman who made me her opening act when she headlined her first tour, where we sang to sold-out stadiums.

She's my ride or die. My soul sister. And yet, even now, I'm lying by omission. Because I haven't told her just how bad things are with the man I'll continue to call the Worst Human Alive.

Swamped by a wave of guilt, I open my mouth to tell her the truth. But I snap it shut again at the sound of creaking floorboards in the other room. We spin at the tap of footsteps at the entry to the kitchen and find her husband Ford Hall—who also happens to own the label I owe music too—holding their five-month-old son Nash against his chest. "You ready to go?"

"Yes," Lake says.

At the same time, I mutter, "I think I should leave."

My best friend turns her blue eyes on me, mouth turned down in a frown. "You aren't leaving."

Her husband shifts a squirming Nash in his arms and studies me. I've known Ford for years. I signed with him before Lake did, in fact. In a strange turn of events, when she did sign with Hall records, she went on to date his son Paul. Oddly, the father and son could not be any more different. While Paul was an unmotivated man child who didn't believe in fidelity—though he's come around recently, I've heard—Ford Hall is one of the most devoted people I've ever met. That extends to his clients and his wife.

Which is good. If not, I'd have to hurt him. Even if he is like a dad to me. Kind of weird considering my best friend now calls him Daddy, but it's fun to tease her about it.

"I agree with Lake."

I snort, even as my heart sinks. "Of course you do."

Lake bites her famous red lips and smiles.

Shit. It's pointless to argue with the two of them. Ford will do whatever makes Lake happy. Happy wife, happy life and all that jazz.

"It's the holidays. You should be with family for the holidays," Lake starts, stepping up beside me and squeezing my hand.

Just the thought of my family has me taking a step back.

Ford is on my other side now, gently cupping my elbow. "And you're family. Right Nash?" he adds in that higher tone people only reserve for babies.

"Of course he's right," Lake replies in a similar tone as she pulls me into a hug.

"Oh my gosh, you're squeezing me so tight I can hardly breathe," I whine, though I snuggle into my best friend's chest.

With a chuckle, Ford presses a kiss to my forehead, then steps back. "We'll always be here for you, Mel. I know you don't want to stay here—"

I shake my head. While Lake doesn't know the extent of what's going on, I couldn't hide it as easily from Ford. Since the Worst Human Alive is my agent, I had to inform Ford that I'd fired him, so he found out pretty quickly that things had gone south. If only the jerk would listen to a word I said and accept that he's been relieved of his position.

"I appreciate you reaching out to your friend. Staying at his house will be just fine."

"I really wish you'd just stay here." Lake pushes her bottom lip out in a dramatic pout.

"Nah, I heard my roomie is a hottie," I say with a shake of my head, trying to lighten the mood. I've always been the wiseass of the two of us. The tease. The girl with a smile. I refuse to allow my ex to steal that too.

Ford snorts. "Who told you that?"

I point to Lake, who merely shrugs. "What? Obviously, I like older men."

Her husband, who is the definition of a silver fox, pulls her into his side and nuzzles her neck. "You're going to pay for calling me old, Red."

She winks at me, then turns a haughty eye at him, mindlessly grasping Nash's wrist gently when he tugs on her hair. "Who said I was talking about you? I was referring to our fire chief, broody Declan Everhart."

Just the sound of his name stirs a sensation to life inside me. Maybe it's the promise of a new beginning, or the thrill of letting go. All I know is that, in this moment, I decide I'm not going to live in the past anymore.

"Okay, family," I tease. "Tell me more about this chief."

ACKNOWLEDGMENTS

Well I think we can all agree, that was hot.

Honestly, this book was just pure fun to write. After the epic love story that was Jay and Cat, and the heartbreakingly beautiful love that Ellie and Frank brought us in Irish, I needed this.

So thank you for an absolutely epic year.

An extra special thank you to Brittanee's Book Babes, my street team. The support you all show me is only rivaled by the support you show one another and I love it.

Thank you to my wonderful beta readers, Becca, Anna, Jenni and Sara, your love for these characters and your insight is so appreciated. And to Amy who is always there to read, listen and highlight all the pages so that everyone can hear these beautiful words in audio. And to the Author Agency and KU Steamy Romance Reads, thank you for your help in promoting this book.

To Beth, my wonderful editor and friend who gets emails from me saying, *hey can we squeeze in a book by the end of the year, oh wait maybe two?* I adore you and appreciate all your help in making my words better.

To Ali, thank you for the gorgeous cover. It fits Ford and Lake perfectly.

And to Sara, *I want to thank me.* LOL. No, I want to thank you. Always. Without you, I would quite literally lose my mind and I'd hate this. You make this all more fun. Even if I make you consider quitting daily.

Last, but never least, to my family and friends who love me in spite of this world that has taken over my life. I love you all.

Now, who is ready to meet our next billionaire and spend more time with the Langfield brothers? Make sure to follow me on Instagram and join my reader group on Facebook.

https://www.facebook.com/groups/brittsboozybookbabes

And don't forget to subscribe to my newsletter!

Lots of love!

ALSO BY BRITTANÉE NICOLE

Bristol Bay Rom Coms

She Likes Piña Coladas

Kisses Sweet Like Wine

Over the Rainbow

Bristol Bay Romance

Love and Tequila Make Her Crazy

A Very Merry Margarita Mix-Up

Boston Billionaires

Whiskey Lies

Loving Whiskey

Wishing for Champagne Kisses

Dirty Truths

Extra Dirty

Mother Faker

(Mother Faker is Book 1 of the Mom Com Series, but is also a lead in to the Revenge Games alongside Revenge Era. This book can be read as a Standalone, or after Revenge Era and before Pucking Revenge)

Revenge Games

Revenge Era

Pucking Revenge

A Major Puck Up

Boston Bolts Hockey

Hockey Boy

Trouble

Standalone Romantic Suspense

Deadly Gossip

Irish

80d984a9-96a2-4f7b-be20-dd993ac78b82R01